"My brother's l[...]

As those words drifted a[...] people all around him sc[...] ready to run for the door. A couple of the women in the restaurant were beginning to cry. From the corner of his eye, Clint could see Mandy standing as still as a statue not five feet from his side.

There were too many people in here.

If guns started going off, one of these folks would catch a bullet just for being in the wrong place at the wrong time. Clint could tell by the way Lee was swaying from side to side that he was fighting to keep from falling over. The look in his eyes was one of nervous anger. Lee wouldn't fall over . . . not unless he was knocked over . . . and not before he tried to do as much damage as he could. Clint knew the man would have absolutely no regard for any of the innocent people sitting and standing by.

"To hell with all of ya!" Lee screamed as his hand went for the gun at his side.

Cursing under his breath, Clint committed himself to the only choice left open to him and threw himself in front of Lee's gun. . . .

DON'T MISS THESE
ALL-ACTION WESTERN SERIES
FROM THE BERKLEY PUBLISHING GROUP

THE GUNSMITH by J. R. Roberts
Clint Adams was a legend among lawmen, outlaws, and ladies. They called him . . . the Gunsmith.

LONGARM by Tabor Evans
The popular long-running series about U.S. Deputy Marshal Long—his life, his loves, his fight for justice.

SLOCUM by Jake Logan
Today's longest-running action Western. John Slocum rides a deadly trail of hot blood and cold steel.

BUSHWHACKERS by B. J. Lanagan
An action-packed series by the creators of Longarm! The rousing adventures of the most brutal gang of cutthroats ever assembled—Quantrill's Raiders.

DIAMONDBACK by Guy Brewer
Dex Yancey is Diamondback, a southern gentleman turned con man when his brother cheats him out of the family fortune. Ladies love him. Gamblers hate him. But nobody pulls one over on Dex . . .

WILDGUN by Jack Hanson
Will Barlow's continuing search for his daughter, kidnapped by the Blackfeet Indians who slaughtered the rest of his family.

THE GUNSMITH 237

THE KILLER CON

J. R. ROBERTS

JOVE BOOKS, NEW YORK

This is a work of fiction. Names, characters, places, and incidents are
either the product of the author's imagination or are used fictitiously,
and any resemblance to actual persons, living or dead, business
establishments, events, or locales is entirely coincidental.

THE KILLER CON

A Jove Book / published by arrangement with
the author

PRINTING HISTORY
Jove edition / September 2001

ONE

"You son of a bitch!"

It wasn't the first time Smitty Evanston had said those words. It wasn't even the first time he'd said them to this particular man. It was, however, the first time he'd said them with a gun in his hand.

Smitty was normally a quiet man. A retired miner with a face full of gray whiskers and a belly full of whiskey, the stocky old man gritted his teeth and began to tremble as the rage that had been building up inside him over the last several months came to a boil. He could feel his anger like a cold steel pit in his stomach, and when he opened his mouth, the profane epithets just seemed to spill out of him as his eyes clouded over with a haze of red.

"I swear to God and all that's holy," Smitty said as his hand wrapped around the pistol he'd cleaned and oiled a few days ago for just such an occasion, "if you don't take back what you said, you'll be layin' dead on yer back inside of a minute."

Shifting on his feet, Owen Respit stared at the older man the way he might look at a child throwing a temper tantrum. Dull brown eyes shifted between Smitty's twitching mouth and the gun in his hand. "Hell, Smitty," Owen said. "I didn't mean to get you all riled up." Taking a few steps back, he added, "It ain't my fault if I heard your wife would spread

1

her legs for less than the price of a cold steak."

Smitty held the gun in a hand shaking with rage. "You take that back."

Owen shrugged. "Take back which one? When I called your wife a dirty whore or when I said she was a cheap, dirty whore?"

The corners of Smitty's eyes twitched furiously as his thumb fumbled to pull back the hammer of his pistol. The weapon was heavy in his hand and at first, he didn't have enough strength to cock it properly. On the second try, the hammer snapped into place, causing Smitty to smile with a crazy gleam in his eye. "What you got to say now, Owen? Any more bigmouth comments for me?"

The amused smirk dropped off the other man's face, to be replaced by a look of cold calculation. "Guess I should be scared," he said as his own hand drifted to the gun hanging at his side. "But all I see in front of me is an old man trembling with fear about to piss a yellow streak down his leg to match the one he's got runnin' down his back."

Smitty's hand stopped trembling and his heart skipped a beat. When he'd bought this gun, he'd never really thought he would be using it as anything more than a showpiece. Now that the time was here, the weapon felt almost too heavy for him to lift. The steel was warming inside his sweaty palms, and it gave off the pungent smell of oil and powder.

There was a crowd gathering around the two men, made up of people who'd seen this feud when it first began and were anxious to see how it ended. Although none of the gathered townspeople wanted to see Smitty die, they were reluctant to turn away from what could be a perfectly good spectacle.

For the next few seconds, Smitty and Owen simply looked at each other, as if from across their front yards. Their faces had lost any trace of anger, and now showed nothing but weary resignation. Owen had yet to clear leather, but his hand rested upon the butt of his gun, waiting to pluck it from its holster and go to work. The tip of Smitty's barrel wavered slightly in front of him.

"I swear," Owen sneered, "that wife of yours musta

plucked them balls straight out from between your legs and—"

Gunfire exploded in the heavy air, blasting through Owen's words before he could even get them all out of his mouth. The sarcastic grin was still on the younger man's face as smoke from his gun curled up in front of his body like a ghostly snake. The pistol in his hand dropped down to point at the ground once it had delivered its round, until it finally slipped from his hand to land with a solid thump at his feet.

Smitty Evanston looked back at him with wide, staring eyes. The shakes were coming back into his muscles, and he suddenly felt as though he'd lost the strength to keep himself upright. His finger was still clutched tightly around the trigger, and he doubted that he could let up on the pressure no matter how much he wanted to drop the weapon and wash the feel of it from his hands for good.

He couldn't believe what he was seeing. The gun smoke curled up from both men's pistols. Owen Respit stared back at him with those beady eyes that Smitty had come to hate over the last several months. But those weren't the same eyes.

Where before, they'd been filled with pompous arrogance and just plain meanness, now those eyes were cold and getting colder as Owen's life seeped out of the fresh hole in his chest to leave a dark crimson stain on his flannel shirt. After a few more seconds, Owen's mouth opened to let out a slow gasp. His hands dropped limply to his sides, and the rest of his body collapsed as though the strings holding him up had suddenly been cut.

Smitty watched all this like a bystander peeking out from one of the surrounding windows. He forgot about the gun in his hand, as well as the wild shot that had been set off by Owen's twitching finger to kick up a pile of dirt near Smitty's left boot. He could still hear the gunshots ringing in his ears and could still feel the pistol bucking in his hand like a living thing.

"Oh, my God," he whispered as the world began moving at its regular pace around him. "Oh, my . . . God."

At that moment, Smitty couldn't tell what upset him the most: the fact that he'd just killed a man, or the fact that he'd fully expected himself to be the one lying dead on the ground after the smoke had cleared.

Looking around, he tried to think about what he should do next. Visions jumped through his mind of judges and nooses, jail cells and courtrooms. He could hear voices around him and people milling about, venturing closer to the grisly scene. Most of the voices were just as surprised as he was, but some of them were angry.

"Smitty went crazy!" one of the bystanders shouted. "All Owen did was poke fun at him."

As much as he wanted to look around and explain himself to the growing crowd of frightened and excited faces, his brain screamed at him to get away before the horrible situation got any worse. And as much as he wanted to pretend that none of this had just happened, Smitty could do nothing else besides tuck the gun into his old belt . . . and run.

TWO

Clint Adams rode into Chester, Utah, just as the sun was sinking below the horizon. The sky was a dark shade of red and the air was beginning to lose some of the heat that had been building up after a day of all sun and no wind. He'd been riding south from Salt Lake City on his way to Arizona, allowing Eclipse to go as fast or as slow as the horse felt like running. Clint was in no particular hurry. In fact, he was certain the man he was going to see wouldn't be going anywhere anytime soon.

Chester was a town that made its living off desperate miners and saloon owners. The place had the feel of a town that had been built on high hopes that had since dropped down lower than the mined-out holes that had been chipped in the surrounding hills. Chester was all it would ever be—a town filled with those who were too tired to move on to someplace better.

Just riding into the town limits, Clint started to feel his own eyelids begin to droop. The streets were quiet. The people sitting outside the buildings were quiet. And the body in the middle of the street . . . that was quiet too.

At first, Clint didn't see the dead man lying facedown in the dirt. When Eclipse came up closer to it, the corpse seemed more like a pile of dirty clothes than a man. Clint had seen more than his share of dead bodies, but this one seemed strange. Mainly because the people nearby simply kept their distance from it, minding their own business. They seemed almost reluctant to interrupt the body's slumber.

Bringing Eclipse to a halt, Clint swung down from the saddle and approached the body, which looked to be a man in his thirties. It didn't take much investigation to discover the blood-caked hole on the front of his shirt. Clint stooped down to look at the dead man's face, but stopped when a voice shouted out from one of the buildings across the street.

"Get away from him!"

Clint straightened and turned to see who'd spoken. Standing in front of a building marked by the swinging shingle bearing the name of Dr. E. Turley was a spindly scarecrow of a man. The word *coot* came to mind right away when Clint saw the old man's crooked posture and the bitter scowl on his dry, wrinkled face.

"Doesn't this town have an undertaker?" Clint asked.

The old coot stepped forward, grunting as he hopped down from the boardwalk and onto the dusty street. He was careful to keep his distance from the body "Sure, we do. But there ain't nobody that wants to join that boy, which is just what'll happen if anyone lays a finger on him."

"Says who?"

Squinting up at Clint, the old man twisted his mouth as though he was sucking on a rotten egg. "You heard of the Respit brothers?"

"No."

"Then you must not be from around here."

"Look," Clint said as the entire day's ride seemed to catch up with him at once. "Cleaning up bodies isn't my business. If you people don't mind the smell, then I'll just make sure to stay somewhere downwind from here."

Without waiting for an answer, Clint led Eclipse around the mess in the street and toward the nearest place that looked like it served food. The establishment was a bit too big to be just a restaurant, but not big enough to be much of a saloon. It was simply called Mil's and at this time of day, it looked far from full.

After tying his reins around a post next to a slope-backed mule, Clint gave Eclipse a scratch behind the ears and walked inside Mil's. The place seemed even smaller on the inside. Not much more than a single room, Mil's contained five round tables and a small bar. There was a young woman sitting at one of the tables in the back of the room, leaning back in her chair with her feet propped up next to an empty place setting.

"Have a seat anywhere you like," she said when Clint walked inside. "You want something to drink?"

Clint picked the table closest to hers, and sat down with his back to the wall in a rickety chair that seemed to groan beneath his weight. "A beer would be nice. What do you have by way of food?"

"We got some chickens that were killed this morning," she said while slowly getting to her feet. "That and some biscuits is about as good as we can do before the cook shows up."

The girl had smooth, lightly tanned skin and a taut, slender body. She wore a simple blue dress that clung to her figure just enough to let Clint see the gentle curves and the slow twitch of her hips as she walked toward the back of the room. Her hair was black with the occasional streak of brown, and fell around her shoulders, curling slightly at the ends. She looked to be in her late twenties, but had the weary eyes of an older woman. When she leaned over the small bar, she pushed her hips out and then glanced over her shoulder, knowing full well where Clint's eyes would be focused.

"Just passing through?" she asked with a sly grin.

Rather than turn his attention away from her body, Clint simply moved his gaze upward until he was looking into her cinnamon-colored eyes. "You got that right. Any town that leaves their dead out in the open isn't a place that I want to stay for very long."

The girl started laughing as she filled up a glass mug from an old beer tap. "Yeah, well, you missed all the excitement about that," she said in a deep voice that had the texture of hard liquor. "The Respits threatened to gun down anyone who so much as touched the body of their brother, and not a lot of folks around here liked Owen enough to risk that kind of trouble over burying him."

Clint waited for her to set the beer down in front of him

before declaring, "I take it these Respits are trouble?"

"You could say that." She peered down at him with a
knowing look in her eyes. She wore a smile that turned her
pale, pink lips up at the corners, bringing out dimples that
shaved a few years off her apparent age. "You want that
chicken or would you rather wait for the cook?"

Taking a moment to get a better look at her, Clint could
tell that this girl was no stranger to having a man's eyes
roaming over her body. The pale blue material of her dress
strained over her rounded hips, which curved up gracefully
along her figure toward small, pert breasts. Her hands looked
strong, but soft. Through the formfitting clothing, Clint could
make out the finely muscled tone of her young shape. By the
time he looked up to her face again, she was smiling warmly.
It was then that he knew that she'd been looking him over
just as carefully.

"How long for the cook to get here?" he asked.

"Long enough for me to join you for that drink."

"Which drink?"

"The one you were about to buy for me."

Clint laughed as he pushed out the chair next to him with
the toe of his boot. "You know, this town is looking better
and better the longer I stay. My name's Clint Adams."

The young woman extended a soft hand, squeezing Clint's
with a grip that showed not only strength but confidence as
well. "Mandy Premont," she said while settling into the chair.
"And believe me, you made a good decision in not letting
me get near that stove."

THREE

Lee Respit sat in the back of a darkened building that used to be one of Chester's three Chinese laundries. The place still smelled of bleach and lye, which only added to the euphoria brought about by the narcotics being consumed in the dark room. There were empty racks hanging along the walls, and rusty tubs stacked in one corner of the cramped quarters. The wooden planks of the floor were weakened by overexposure to moisture, which caused the occasional footstep to crash all the way through to the soil beneath the structure.

The place wasn't completely barren, though. Since the laundry had closed, one of the Chinese owners had put in a few cots, hung some paper figures from the ceiling, and tossed some cheap rugs onto the floor to turn it into an opium den. Catering to those in town who were willing to pay the price for their escape from reality, the Chinese owner was making more money now than when the place had been full of starched shirts and folding tables.

Reclining on a tattered mattress with stuffing spilling out from countless holes, Lee Respit brought the copper pipe to his lips and took a long pull of acrid smoke into his lungs. He held it inside himself, thought about his brother who was rotting outside, and let it seep out from between clenched teeth. He was big enough to take up most of the mattress. His chest was wide, yet sunken in from a childhood disease

9

that had nearly claimed his life. Lee's father had always told him that it was that disease that had made Lee so much stronger than his brothers.

Lee had always wondered how his father could say things like that only a few hours after beating him within an inch of his life.

But that was a long time ago. Now, as he took another pull from the communal pipe set up in the corner of the shadowy opium den, Lee Respit could only think of his dead brother lying out in the street for everyone to see. He hadn't let anyone take the body away because he'd wanted the town to watch Owen rot for a while and wonder about the vengeance that was coming to make up for what that old fool Smitty had done.

There was going to be hell to pay, that was certain. And if his father had taught Lee anything, it was that waiting for the whipping made the punishment seem that much worse.

Sitting on the floor next to Lee, with his back propped up against the wall, was Nickolas Respit. He was the youngest of the brothers and the one who seemed to be taking Owen's death worse than anyone. The eighteen-year-old's fair hair and clean-shaven cheeks seemed to work together to make the ugly patch of burned skin down the side of his neck seem that much worse.

Nickolas had been crying for the better part of an hour, although his tears were mostly due to the drugs in his system rather than the grief in his heart. "What are we gonna do, Lee?" he whined between puffs.

Lee watched the smoke circle his head before letting his eyes fall to his brother's level. "I'm gonna sit here and finish my smoke. Let everyone get a good, long look at Owen. Let them see what that old man did."

"Pa wouldn't like us leavin' Owen out there like that. He wouldn't like it at all."

Pitching the end of the copper tube to the floor, Lee reached down to send a vicious backhand across his sibling's face. "Shut yer damn mouth." One of the Chinese attendants started to move toward Nickolas, but stopped short when they saw the mean look in Lee's burning eyes. "First of all," Lee snarled, "Pa's dead. And if he'd seen what happened out there today, he would'a gone outside and started beating the tar outta you and me for letting that happen to his favorite son."

"I don't unnerstand," Nickolas said as the drugs took hold of his tongue. "Smitty ain't no killer. Owen was jus funnin' with him and now he's dead. . . ."

"That old man got in a lucky shot, is all. There ain't no more to it than that. But his luck's run out."

Nickolas ignored the throbbing pain in his face where Lee had struck him, and raised his pipe as if to toast his brother's vow. He then suckled the tube without a lick of shame before slumping over dead asleep two minutes later.

Lee never picked his pipe back up, however. Instead, he sat forward with his elbows propped up on his knees and began trying to get his wits about him. He thought about his brothers, one dead and the other not too far behind, and then thought about the words his father would have for him if he were still alive.

"It was a lucky shot, Pa," Lee whispered to the churning smoke and the other glazed-over sets of eyes scattered about the room. "I swear, it wasn't nothin' more than dumb luck. We'll set things right. Just you wait and see."

Just over an hour later, Lee Respit walked out of the old laundry and into the nearly empty streets of Chester. He was surprisingly steady on his feet for the amount of time he'd spent among the opium fumes, and when he drew his gun, it was with a slow, deliberate hand.

It wasn't late, but the sun had long since gone. A trickle of moonlight dripped from a cloudy sky to fall upon the tops of houses and the deserted boardwalks. After rounding a corner, he came within sight of the crumpled form of his brother's body, which hadn't been touched by anything besides the occasional breeze.

Owen looked peaceful, despite the condition he was in. Looking down at the eerily still body, Lee gripped his gun a little tighter and turned to survey the surrounding area. There was a strange horse tied in front of Mil's restaurant, which might have gone unnoticed if it didn't contrast so sharply to the mule next to it. One of Lee's talents was spotting good horses, and there hadn't been any worth stealing in this town for weeks. But that Darley Arabian was a different story. That could fetch a pretty penny without having to look too far for a buyer.

Something else interested him more, however. Something about the horse besides its value. Mainly, Lee was interested in the tracks that circled around Owen's body and then led to Mil's. They had to belong to that Darley. And that meant that whoever was riding that horse had been messing around too close to forbidden territory.

Lee felt some of the drugs rattle his brain as he headed toward the restaurant. Violent thoughts flashed through his mind about what he was going to do to whoever had felt the need to gawk at his brother's corpse. He'd wanted the body to sit out there, but had specifically warned folks to keep their distance.

He had his reasons.

Walking with slow, steady steps, Lee made his way across the street and toward the small restaurant. He took deep breaths as he moved, trying to clear some of the fog from his eyes before charging inside. He wasn't afraid of any of the thickheaded locals, or even of the law, but he knew better than to get into a fight without his wits about him.

Pa would've told him to wait until the opium wore off, but Lee knew that would give that asshole inside too much time. Besides, he wouldn't need more than half his speed to get the drop on anyone in there.

FOUR

Clint didn't mind waiting for the cook since Mandy kept him company as she set the other tables and did a little bit of sweeping. Whenever she finished one of her tasks, she would come back to Clint and pull her chair just a little closer as she nursed a warm beer.

"So who are these Respits?" Clint asked while she was preparing for the dinner crowd. "And what have they got against proper burials?"

Shrugging. Mandy busied herself with a handful of napkins and set one at each place setting. "The Respits live out on an old ranch outside of town. They used to raise horses, but now they just keep horses there after they steal them until they can sell them off. They're all nothing but troublemakers and thieves. If they wasn't so sneaky about it, the sheriff would have enough evidence to hang 'em.

"As for that body out there . . . I couldn't tell you much. All I heard is that after Owen got shot and the sheriff refused to arrest the man that did it, Lee about went crazy. Nearly started shooting up the whole town."

"Why didn't the sheriff make an arrest? Was it a fair fight?"

"If you could call it a fight. More like a damn lucky shot. Ol' Smitty just got tired of taking Owen's shit and decided to put an end to it. Hell, most everyone thought it would be

13

him layin' dead in the street instead of Owen."

The story wasn't a new one to Clint. Sometimes even the most experienced gunmen lost out to plain bad luck. Guns jammed or went off when they shouldn't. A sound was missed that turned out to be footsteps creeping up from behind. Or sometimes the most unlikely opponent became the last man a gunman would ever face. When life and death were at stake, lots of strange factors got thrown into the mix. And though Clint would put his money down on skill over luck any day of the week, he would never deny that fate's twists were definitely part of the equation.

Just then, the front door opened and a dark-skinned man wearing a battered leather jacket entered the place. Without giving Clint or Mandy much more than a second glance, he took off his jacket, hung it on a hook, and plucked a stained apron from one of the racks. He tied it around his waist and headed for the kitchen. The cook was a portly Indian with a long black ponytail tied behind his head and a red bandanna knotted around his neck. After disappearing into the next room, he mumbled to himself and moved pots and pans noisily from cabinets and shelves.

Mandy had given herself a break and was sitting next to Clint again. She sighed heavily and set down her beer. "When he starts making all that noise, I'm supposed to jump up and get to work."

"Getting ready for the dinner rush?" Clint asked.

"It usually isn't that much of a rush," she said while getting to her feet. "That's why I don't really take this job all that seriously." Leaning down to Clint's ear, she added, "I think that's what gets the cook so upset. Give him a few minutes, though, and he'll be ready to fix your supper."

The door opened again, this time to let in a couple in their fifties who waved to Mandy and sat down at one of the tables in the front.

"Before you get too busy," Clint said, "can I ask you one more thing?"

"Sure."

"Are there many other visitors in town?"

She thought about that for a second and nodded. "I can think of a few. There's a couple that came in on a stage from

Wyoming a few days ago and are waiting for the line to Nebraska. There's another visitor, but he shouldn't concern you too much, I'd guess."

"Who is it?"

"Just some huckster that rolled into town last week. He got caught trying to sell deeds to mines that didn't even exist to some of the local miners. He's cooling his heels in the sheriff's jail right now, waiting for Judge Christian to get back from Salt Lake."

"You didn't happen to catch a name of that fellow in jail, did you?" Clint asked.

Leaning in close, Mandy took a quick glance toward the kitchen and dropped her voice to a whisper. "I don't remember exactly, but it sounded Injun. Wide Oak or something like that."

Clint stood up and held a few coins out toward the young woman. "Thank you very much, Mandy. This is for the beers and your time."

She didn't even try to hide the disappointment on her face. "Aren't you going to stay for dinner?"

"I'll be back. But first, I've got to pay a visit to a huckster who I haven't seen for quite a while. Is the sheriff's office nearby?"

Mandy gave him directions to where he could find the town's law. Apparently, Sheriff Kenrick had an office one block over on Marker Avenue.

Already, Clint could smell the beginnings of some great meals drifting out from the kitchen. At first whiff, he detected a steak that had just been thrown onto a fire as well as some bread that had probably been set on top of the range to warm. He pushed aside his hunger, however, and assured himself he would be back in a few minutes. Watching Mandy walk over to the older couple at the other table, he came up with another very good reason to come back as soon as possible.

Stepping outside, Clint stood for a few seconds to let his eyes adjust to the darkness that had fallen over the town since he'd walked inside Mil's. The air had taken on a chilling edge that smelled of horses and pine trees. Suddenly, a shadow fell onto Eclipse's side.

Clint's eyes had gotten used to the dark just in time for

him to make out the figure of a man standing next to the hitching post. Whoever it was, he was standing a bit too close to Eclipse for Clint's tastes. "Something I can help you with?" Clint asked.

The shadow man didn't move. "This your horse?"

Taking another step closer, Clint lowered his hand to settle over his pistol. "Sure is. Would you mind giving him a little space? I don't want him getting fidgety."

When the man took a step to the side, Clint could see the vague outline of the crumpled body that was still lying in the middle of the nearby street.

"I'm Lee Respit," the man in the shadows said. "And I'd like to know why you had to ride around my brother over there like he was some goddamn sideshow."

Clint could tell, even in the darkness, that Lee's hand was hovering closer to the gun strapped at his side. Although he didn't shift his own hand, Clint readied himself to move at the first provocation.

"I just got to town," Clint said. "It's not too often you find something like that. I was just making sure he didn't need any help."

The longer the other man stood there, the stronger the smell around him invaded the air. He reeked of smoke and opium. Although Clint knew better than to poison himself with those drugs, he knew that odor well enough after facing plenty of men who didn't follow his precautions. To Clint, that smell meant one thing: a man who would be slower on the draw, but also quicker to start a fight.

Rather than try to engage someone like this in conversation, Clint walked slowly toward his horse and reached out to pat Eclipse on the muzzle. Lee watched tensely, but didn't try to stop him. After a few moments crawled by, the man stepped from the shadows and went inside the restaurant.

Clint listened and watched through the window to make sure the man wasn't going in to start anything besides a meal. Satisfied that things would be all right for the next few minutes, he walked down the street and turned the corner, immediately spotting the sheriff's office on Marker Avenue.

FIVE

The sheriff's office looked like it had once been the home of a small family. Rather than the normal storefront that many towns gave to their lawmen, this one looked as though it had been chosen merely because the building was already there. In fact, Clint had to make sure that he wasn't stepping into somebody's home when he rapped on the door and pushed it open.

Inside, the place looked much more like what Clint was expecting. There was a desk next to a small window, and another at the opposite end of the room. The bigger of the two was the one closest to the door. Sitting there was a young man who obviously had some Mexican blood running through his veins. He looked up at Clint with focused eyes. Short black hair was neatly trimmed around a face that gave him the appearance of someone much too young to be in a lawman's boots.

"Hello," Clint said as he stepped inside. "I'm looking for the sheriff."

The young man got up and raised to his full six feet two inches. The gleaming silver badge seemed almost out of place pinned to a simple red and black flannel shirt. "You found him," he said in a resonating voice. The sheriff extended a pawlike hand and shook Clint's with an obvious show of strength. "I'm Wes Kenrick. You're new in town, aren't you?"

Clint had to respect the other man's grip, but shook his head at the way the sheriff seemed so desperate to display it. "That's right, Sheriff," Clint said while making sure to hold the posturing youth's eyes. "The name's Clint Adams."

"Clint Adams? I heard of you. Never thought I'd get to meet you in person, though. What brings you to Chester?"

"Actually, I'd like to see one of the men you've got in your jail. I heard you've got ahold of someone who was trying to cheat some of the miners in the area."

Sheriff Kenrick nodded. "Yeah, we caught him, all right. Actually, I didn't do more than bring him in. Lucky thing too. The folks that did catch on to his little scheme wanted to string him up on the spot. I thought I was gonna have to start shooting to bring the lying crook in alive."

"Did you get his name?"

"Sure did. Fella calls himself Henry Whiteoak."

Kenrick stepped around his desk and stood in front of the door with his thumbs hooked beneath his gunbelt. "Can I ask why someone like you would be interested in a two-bit cheat?"

That was the same question Clint had been asking himself the entire time he'd been riding through Utah. He still hadn't come up with much of an answer. "Well, I haven't seen him for some time, but I heard he was in the area and figured he'd be up to no good. Looks like I was right."

Kenrick shook his head and turned around to open the door behind him. Reaching out, he plucked a key ring from a hook on the wall, and led the way down a narrow hallway that led straight back to the rear of the building. The hall had a brick wall on one side and a row of three steel-barred cages on the other. A fat man wearing a nightshirt lay sprawled out on a cot in the first cell. Even from outside the cage, Clint could pick up the stench of whiskey that hung around the drunk like a thick cloud.

They kept walking, past the empty middle cell, until they reached the last one in line. Inside, there was a man who sat with his back propped up against the bars and his legs crossed in front of him as though he was relaxing on his own front porch rather than languishing in the custody of the law.

"Look sharp, fast-talker," Sheriff Kenrick said while slamming his fist against the bars and rattling the prisoner's head. "You got a visitor."

"Thank you, Sheriff," Clint said.

The lawman held out his hand. "I'll have to ask you for your gun, Mr. Adams. Just as long as you're with the prisoners."

Clint removed his pistol and handed it over to the sheriff. "I won't be long," he said.

Kenrick took the gun and held it with a kind of gentle reverence. He walked back into his office, leaving the door wide open behind him.

All this time, the prisoner hadn't moved a muscle. Instead, he waited until the sheriff's footsteps had died away before tilting his head to the side and slapping his knees with both hands. "Did I hear that boy mention Clint Adams?" Swinging his legs over the side of the cot, the prisoner turned around to face Clint, wearing a look of complete amazement. "I don't suppose the mighty Gunsmith has come to break me out of this backwater town?"

"Not hardly," Clint said. "Actually, I was thinking the sheriff might need another person's testimony to put you out of business for good. Maybe even a helping hand to help build the gallows."

That brought the prisoner to his feet and wiped the self-satisfied smile off his face. Although he was a few years older and a bit rough around the edges, Henry Whiteoak still looked as Clint had remembered. Standing just under six feet tall, the man wore his dark brown hair clean cut to match his smooth cheeks, giving him the kind of face that most folks tended to trust . . . right until they found out every bit of money had been swindled out of their pockets.

SIX

Whiteoak wore a white tailored shirt with the sleeves rolled up around sinewy arms. Clint had met up with the con man once several years ago, but had never been able to forget the encounter. At the time, Whiteoak had been on the run from a land baron and his hired assassins over a real estate swindle. Clint had gotten wrapped up in the mess, and Whiteoak was a big help in getting it all straightened out. Still, that didn't mean that the lanky man was to be trusted.

Clint leaned against the brick wall and stared into the cage, truly enjoying the sight of Whiteoak behind bars. "Still selling snake oil from the back of that old wagon? Or have you been making your living cheating at cards?"

Reaching up to tug at the string tie around his neck, Whiteoak nodded and tried to regain the composure he'd lost at having to deal from the inside of a jail cell. "I'm sure you're getting a kick out of this, Adams. Did you track me down to laugh in my face, or did you have something else in mind?"

"What made you think I had to track you down? You still haven't learned how not to attract attention."

"What then? Need a few fashion tips?" Whiteoak fell into his normal character and strutted about inside his cage as though it was his living room. "That riding gear doesn't suit someone of your fame. You should loosen the purse strings a bit. Get some nice suits like your friend Bat Masterson. Now he's got some style."

Clint took a step forward and stared directly into Whiteoak's eyes. "You know what your problem is? You still don't know when to shut up."

The words hung in the air between the two men. They were simple enough, but more than adequate to wipe the smirk off Whiteoak's face. After a few seconds, the prisoner threw up his hands and plopped back down onto the cot.

"All right then," Whiteoak said. "What do you want?"

"I want you to tell me what kind of shit you've stirred up in this town."

Glancing over his shoulder, Whiteoak somehow managed to look genuinely offended by Clint's words. "I beg your pardon?"

"First of all, I heard about the con you were pulling back in Wyoming."

Whiteoak's hurt expression gave way to a fond smile. "Ah, yes. That was a beaut."

"Yeah . . . right up until they put the price on your head and chased you out of town."

"Have you been checking up on me?"

"No, but as soon as I got in these parts, I began hearing about some con man who's stealing everything that isn't nailed down. Stories like that aren't too rare, but it seems this particular con man has a way of knocking people out with the concoctions he sells them before waltzing in and taking all their money. Combine that with the cheating at cards and I'm reminded of the last time we met." Clint shook his head like a disapproving parent. "You'd think since the last time I had to save that lying ass of yours, you'd have at least changed your game around a bit. Even a dog knows when it's time to find a new yard."

"Jesus, Adams, you'd think someone like you would have better things to do than keep track of a hustler working his trade with a bunch of rubes."

"Well, you just happened to catch me in between, so actually I don't have a lot else to do right now. Besides, since the trail you left only branched off of mine by about a day's ride, I decided to come by and make sure you weren't leading another group of angry killers around from town to town."

Clint reached through the bars and grabbed hold of Whiteoak's collar. With one sharp motion, he pulled the other man up against the bars until his face was jammed into the steel.

"Oh, and there's one other thing," Clint said with an angry sneer. "Maybe you can explain why all those people who talked about you also mentioned that I was riding alongside of you. Got any quick answers for that little mystery?"

Whiteoak clenched his eyes shut as if expecting his face to get slammed against steel one more time. "Uhhh . . . that's awful strange. . . ."

Clint obliged by shoving the con man's head back a little before pulling it forcefully into the bars. "I don't like that answer." *Slam*. "Try again."

"Mass hallucinations?"

Leaning into the cell, Clint got ready to give the con man another bruise to add to his collection, but Whiteoak's voice stopped him before he heard the dull thump of bone against metal.

"All right, all right!" the prisoner shouted.

Clint looked down the hall to find Sheriff Kenrick poking his head into the corridor. The lawman must have been holding Whiteoak for longer than Clint had thought, since he didn't do anything to stop the prisoner from getting his head knocked around. Once Clint held up his hands to show that he wasn't holding a weapon, the sheriff gave a casual wave and walked back to his desk.

"I see you make friends as quick as ever, Whiteoak. Now what were you about to say?"

"I may have dropped your name a few times . . . just to tell about the excitement we went through. Everyone likes hearing about gunfights and things like that. Plus, it's always good to have friends if people come charging after you with murder on their minds."

"Even if those friends are nothing but smoke and hot air coming out of your mouth?"

Whiteoak shrugged. "A technicality."

Letting go of Whiteoak's collar, Clint stepped back and

let out a heavy sigh. "What did you do to wind up in there?"

"Nothing fancy. Just a few documents to some mines I acquired in a game of faro not too long ago. It's not my fault the man who lost them was a scoundrel wanted for forgery in three states."

"What else?"

The lanky man inside the cell began rubbing his temples with his fingertips. "There ain't nothing else."

"Something just doesn't sit right with all this," Clint said. "You may be a con artist, but you're a better one than this. Why get so sloppy all of a sudden and leave a trail that leads from here to Wyoming?"

"Maybe I'm slipping in my old age."

"I thought about that myself. But you're not that old. No," Clint said as he walked up and grabbed the bars with both hands. "There's more to it than that. How long have you been using my name?"

Whiteoak said nothing.

"You knew I was in the area, didn't you?" Clint pressed.

Finally, Whiteoak looked up and dropped the innocent act that had become his second nature. "You're not that hard to find either," he said. "People talk about you after you leave town. I wanted to get ahold of you and I highly doubted you would've responded to a telegram." After straightening his tie, Whiteoak got back to his feet and leaned in close to the bars. "I need your help, Adams. I think you're the only one that can keep me alive."

SEVEN

Lee Respit sat at a table in the back of Mil's, ordered a beer, and waited.

He sat there and thought about the look on that stranger's face. The one who'd looked down on his brother's body like it wasn't anything but a piece of meat. The one who'd looked at Lee like he was less than a man. Like Lee was something beneath him.

The longer he sat in the restaurant, the madder Lee became. He wanted to kill that stranger, for no better reason than for the look he'd given him in passing. After Lee switched to water, he could feel the opium's effects wearing off.

Most men who drew off those pipes leaned back like they were flying off to somewhere else. Somewhere better than the place they'd left behind. But not Lee. When he took that acrid smoke into his chest, he felt himself get pulled inside his own heart, where he was forced to look at his soul up close. What he saw was not a place he liked to go, but it was somewhere he needed to be sometimes so that he could be reminded of who he was.

He was a violent man who could hear the screams within himself when he was forced to look hard enough. He was a killer who could hear the dying breaths of every man whose life he'd ended. When he heard those things, Lee knew it

24

was too late to turn away . . . too late to repent as Pa would have wanted.

He went to the opium dens when he needed to see those things. Especially when he was about to listen to another man's dying breaths.

Smitty Evanston was not a lucky man. Not normally anyway.

Most of his life had been a continual series of setbacks like the one that had stranded him in the town of Chester, Utah. He'd been ready to search for his fortune in California when the man sponsoring his trip out west had died at the bottom of the very mine that Smitty had been hired to work.

At the time, his wife had told him that he was lucky not to have been there when that tunnel collapsed. For a while, Smitty had agreed. But as the years went on and he became poorer and poorer, Smitty knew that his luck was just plain bad. Any bit of money he would come into dried up like an old riverbed. Any job he was offered wound up going to someone else. Any day he woke up feeling good about his life ended with a splitting headache.

His ultimate stroke of bad luck had started when Owen Respit began tormenting him as some kind of cruel hobby. It had started out small, with a couple of shoves in the dry goods store and some rude comments from across the saloon. Then, the shoves had become beatings, and Smitty had known from experience that it would only get worse from there.

And it had . . . until that medicine man had rolled into town.

Professor Whiteoak drove in a few days ago in a wagon painted up like it had wandered away from a circus. Big letters written in bright red paint on the canvas sides proclaimed, "Professor Whiteoak's Amazing Cure-All Tonic—10 cents a bottle to cure whatever ails you."

Thinking back to that day, Smitty swore he could still hear the professor's melodious voice crying out to anyone who would listen. "Come one, come all. The miracle of miracles. The splendor of modern science. It's all here. Give me a few moments of your time and your life will be changed forever."

After a few minutes of that, the professor had gathered

himself quite a crowd. And as soon as he had an audience
big enough to suit him, the professor went on about the miracles his tonic could perform.

Everything ranging from heartaches to stomach cramps,
indigestion to the common cold, chills, fevers, and sore
throats, all of it could be cured by administering the tonic.
Smitty was no fool. He didn't believe a word of it . . . not
until he saw some hunched-over old man take a drink of the
stuff and then begin dancing around like he was a spry young
boy.

Mrs. Peters bought a bottle for her headaches, and said
she could feel the stuff running through her body like it was
cleaning away every bit of pain she had. Needless to say,
those bottles were getting snatched up as fast as people could
fish a dime from their pockets, but Smitty still had his res-
ervations.

He'd waited until the crowd was thinning out before he
made his way up to the professor and pulled him aside. The
man carried himself like he'd been to a real school, and
talked with words that Smitty hadn't even heard before, but
not once did Whiteoak treat him as anything less than an
equal.

"Professor," Smitty said those several days ago, "I got
something that you might not have a tonic for. It ain't so
much a medical problem, but a stretch of bad luck. I got debt
I can't never pay and men in town that beat on me like I
was the runt of their litter."

Whiteoak finished up taking the money from a young man
with bad eyes, and turned to focus all his attention on Smitty.
"My good fellow," the professor said sympathetically, "I
know exactly what you are speaking about. Why, not so long
ago, I suffered from the same ailment as you just described,
which prompted me to concoct a potent mixture which turned
my misfortune into a string of happy days."

Smitty caught the general flow of the other man's speech
so long as he didn't try to figure out every single word. He
watched as the professor took him to a small set of drawers
built into the side of his wagon. With a wink and a flourish
of his hands, Whiteoak had produced a small brass key from
the watch pocket of his red velvet vest.

Even now, sitting by himself, too afraid to light a lamp or even start a fire, Smitty could see that brass key in the professor's hand as though he was still standing in front of that colorful wagon. The little drawers had looked so mysterious. There must have been at least five or six of them, each one protected by its own special lock. Whiteoak fitted the key into one of the top drawers, and pulled it out to reveal a bundle of cloths that completely filled the brick-sized compartment.

He removed the bundle and unwrapped three tiny vials of brown liquid, which looked a little darker than the elixir he'd been selling to the rest of the town. "This, my friend," Whiteoak said while handing over one of the vials, "is the very same potion that turned my luck around and built me into the prosperous specimen you see before you today. Thanks to this tonic coursing through my system, I can earn my living and smite my enemies like a true champion of men."

When Smitty held that vial in his hands, he swore he could feel heat coming through the glass to warm his fingers like sunshine on a windowpane. Even now, the memory of that warmth brought a smile to his face. Just to ease his troubled mind, Smitty dug in his pocket and removed the vial, which was now empty and dry as a bone.

Whiteoak's words echoed in his brain the way a reverend's voice bounced around inside a church. "You too can live the life of the fortunate. Your wife will get that gleam back in her eye and those men that harass you will step aside, recognizing you as their better. Just five dollars, my good man, and this miracle can be yours. Five little dollars to put your entire life back on track."

Smitty barely had more than that at the time, and his hopes fell painfully to the bottom of his stomach. Somehow, Whiteoak sensed this, and a charitable smile lit up his face.

"I'll tell you what, friend. Since I can tell you're someone in dire need of a miracle, I'll do you a favor. Make it one dollar. Trust me, it may seem like a lot of money now, but it will be more than worth it once fate smiles down upon you. In fact, you might find that much lying in the street once your luck takes its turn for the better."

The professor seemed genuinely concerned for him. Even

now, Smitty felt bad for making Whiteoak cut his price down
so drastically. That man would probably have to take a cut
in his budget to make up for the slack, but he'd done it with
a smile on his face simply to help out his fellowman. No
matter how much it hurt Smitty to part with that money, the
old man knew he was making a sound investment.

Holding the vial in his hands, knowing that it was his to
keep and use, Smitty could already feel his luck beginning
to change. Hadn't it been lucky for him to meet up with such
a fine man instead of those hustlers that came through sometimes? Hell, those other salesmen gave men like the professor
a bad name.

"Thank you," Smitty said while Whiteoak locked up the
rest of the special tonic. "Thank you so much."

"Not at all, my good man. The pleasure I'll get from seeing your good fortune will more than make up for what I
lost in the bargain. The good deed was profit enough."

What a kind man, Smitty now thought as he wrapped his
jacket tighter around his body and rubbed his hands together
to keep his fingers from going numb. Such a giving soul.

And Whiteoak was right.

The tonic slid down Smitty's throat and turned his stomach, making him feel the same kind of sick he always felt
whenever he got a taste of molasses. In fact, the stuff actually
tasted like molasses, but a little watery. He knew the potion
had to have been more than molasses because, as soon as he
drank it down, his life began to change.

He could feel a spring in his step that even his wife noticed
when he walked through the door. He could feel the wind in
his hair, and noticed the way others looked at him differently
when he passed. And the day after the professor's exhibition,
Owen Respit started in on him again . . . this time insulting
his wife.

Smitty let it go for a while on account of him feeling so
good. But when he'd had enough, Smitty felt his hand
twitching on the handle of a gun that hadn't killed anything
bigger than a squirrel for years.

That had been yesterday. Fortune had indeed been smiling
upon him, because when he saw that Owen was meaning to
shoot him down, Smitty's hand drew that pistol and went to

work, dropping that son of a bitch in the street like a mangy dog.

Of course, Owen's brothers didn't like that too much, which was why Smitty was hiding anywhere he could in town. That oldest one, Lee, was a crazy man. As soon as Smitty saw him, he'd started running for his life. It must've been the potion's doing that let him find a place to hide when Lee had stormed down the street with a rifle in his hand, looking for whoever had killed his brother.

Lee screamed and screamed. He even said that he wouldn't bury Owen until he could bury Smitty right beside him, and that he'd kill anyone in town that so much as looked at that body. He'd even put a round into poor Ned Zander's son just to prove his point.

"You want it to stop?" Lee screamed. "Then tell me where that bastard is!"

Smitty knew it was only the luck he'd gotten from that vial that was keeping him alive this long. Without it, he'd be lying in the street instead of Owen. By the good graces of Professor Henry Whiteoak, Smitty Evanston was alive to see another day.

He only wished he had another drink of that syrupy luck to see him through tomorrow.

EIGHT

Looking into Henry Whiteoak's eyes, Clint searched for any sign that the con man was trying to put something over on him. It had been a while since he'd met up with the "professor," but Clint remembered well enough how slippery the other man could be. He'd heard Whiteoak's sales pitch, and had even played cards with him. As far as he could tell, however, this time Whiteoak was being completely serious.

"What do you mean, you need my help to keep alive?" Clint asked.

"Just what I said." Leaning in closer to the bars, Whiteoak whispered as though there was somebody close enough to hear them. "I managed to acquire deeds to some gold mines out in California as well as to a few veins of silver around these parts."

"I don't suppose these would be the same mines that you tried to unload when you got arrested and thrown in here?"

Whiteoak dismissed that with a wave of his hand. "Hell, no. Those were stripped-out holes. I needed that money to make the last payment on some equipment I was gonna use to work those claims. What I'm talking about is a real find. This is the type of thing that could make a man rich."

"If these claims are so good, why keep pulling that wagon of yours around? Why not just head for the mines and start digging?"

30

"Because, besides equipment, I need to buy up some property to live on and save up enough to hire protection and a few extra hands. Since I only know one trade, I've been working my way on one last circuit before packing it in for good."

Clint scratched his chin and regarded the professor carefully. Most of his brain told him not to believe a single word that came from Whiteoak's mouth. But there was still that one little piece that worked in the other man's favor. For the moment, he wasn't sure which part to act on. "So let me get this straight. You start dropping my name all over the place, knowing that I'll hear about it eventually. And that started when?"

"That started when I was down in Arizona a month or so back and I heard one of the hotel owners bragging about how he heard you were in town. My own troubles were just starting then, and I got the idea to drop a trail in front of you to follow sort of like the trail you left behind. I knew that'd get your attention."

"And what made you think I'd go through all the trouble of tracking you down?" Clint asked. "And why should I help you now that I did find you?"

"Because I met you, Adams. I may not be an honest man, but I'm a damn good judge of them. You wouldn't let a man die after what we been through. No matter what you thought of me, you wouldn't let another human being get murdered who's only a few towns away. Not if you could help it anyway."

"So who are these men that are after you?"

"Sore losers. That's all."

Clint couldn't help but laugh. "You wouldn't be talking about the rightful owners to those mines that you acquired, would you?" When Whiteoak didn't answer right away, Clint stepped up closer to the cell and rested his hands on the cold steel bars. "You cheat a bunch of miners out of their livelihood and then get all upset when they come to get it back? You ask me, I'd say that you had this coming."

"All right, Adams," Whiteoak hissed. "You want the truth, well, here it is." He stood face-to-face with Clint and squared his shoulders almost as though he was about to draw a gun.

"I won those deeds fair and square. Sure, the poker table was crooked, but not any more crooked than any other table in any other saloon. Everybody cheats at cards, you know that."

As much as Clint wanted to argue that statement, he simply couldn't. While he was no cheat, he'd spotted at least one at every saloon he'd ever been to. It was only the truly skilled gamblers who were the exceptions to the cheating rule. He'd seen some that were so good that it was a miracle they didn't cheat. Doc Holliday sprang to mind in that category.

But for every gambler that relied on luck and skill, there were a hundred that relied on sleight of hand. For those players, it was an accepted fact that cheating happened. The real trick was in not getting caught.

"So there's a lot of cheats out there," Clint said. "So what?"

"Well, I was at a table full of 'em and I still managed to get every last cent out of their pockets," Whiteoak said proudly. "Hell, Adams, the men at that table probably had two spare decks up their sleeves between them. The point is, I won those deeds and went away a rich man. They laughed it off and let me go, taking me for a fool.

"Well, they stopped laughing when I had those mines checked out. It seems everyone in town who worked a pick or pan thought those deeds weren't worth the paper they were written on. Those men at that table thought they'd gotten a night of cards for the price of a few pieces of worthless pulp. But I felt lucky that night, Adams. Truly lucky.

"I had a look into those mines and found a nugget the size of your big toe." Whiteoak's eyes lit up at the thought. He held his hands out as though he still had the smooth rock in his grasp, and rubbed his fingers together as if glittering dust was still beneath his nails. "My guess is that there's something to the rest of them deeds as well. It was probably a mistake that they wound up in a poker game at all.

"Those deeds are mine, Adams. You can check them with the claims office yourself for proof if you want. Now those sore losers are after them, and won't rest until they get those papers back in their hands. My one chance to make an honest living and it'll turn out to be the death of me."

"That's a real sad story there, Professor," Clint said. "Except you seemed to gloss over the fact that you still wound up cheating your way from Arizona to Salt Lake and then back down again. What kind of an honest living is that?"

"I told you before. I needed money to pay for protection before I could ever go near those mines again. I show my face anywhere in that area and someone'll blow it off."

"And this honest living of yours . . ." Clint ran his fingers down the bars and knocked on them with his knuckle. "Were you going to run it from in here?"

"After I left Salt Lake and came here, I got arrested. I figured on staying here since this'd be the safest place for me to be until you showed up."

"And what if I didn't show?"

"Then I'd pay my bail and think of something else. You can check on that too."

Clint shook his head while trying to straighten out the tangled mess that was Whiteoak's story. The more he thought about it, the bigger the headache he got. But there was something inside all the threads that he didn't expect to come from a man like the professor. There was the slightest ring of truth at the core of it all that made Clint wonder if any of what the man was saying could actually be taken at face value.

There was also enough inside the story to catch Clint's interest. He'd ridden with the con man, and had even fought beside him, but he would never consider Whiteoak anything close to a friend. The professor was right about one thing, however. Clint couldn't turn away from an honest plea for help with his conscience still intact. Besides, he also wanted to check on this story, if only to call Whiteoak's bluff.

"All right," Clint finally said. "I'll check into this."

"My wagon's parked behind the livery. There's a set of keys hidden under the rear axle and a secret drawer under the floor below the driver's seat. The deeds are there, along with enough money for me to have bought my way out of here a long time ago." He also talked about a compartment in the wagon's side that contained more important information.

Clint stared the man down until Whiteoak's hopeful expression died off. "I'll check," Clint said, "but I'm warning you . . . it'll take a hell of a lot to convince me that you're not full of shit."

"I'd expect no less."

"And one more thing." Stepping up until he could feel the cold from the bars against his face, Clint looked directly into Whiteoak's eyes and fixed him with a killing stare. "If I find out . . . or even get the slightest hint. . . . that I came all this way for nothing, I'll be after you. And there isn't a jail cell in this country that could keep you safe from me."

NINE

In a town like Chester, which sat out in the open country all by itself, the nighttime sky seemed especially dark. It stretched out overhead, making Clint feel like he was at the bottom of an ocean when he looked straight up to the inky blackness. Countless stars spread out, winking with their own light, and the longer he looked, the more there seemed to be. The sun hadn't just set, but had dropped down below the horizon as if it had slipped from God's fingers.

Times like these were what Clint loved most about being on the trail. If he could just ride out away from town, he could be that much closer to the magnificent stars and away from the headaches that came along with people like Henry Whiteoak and these Respit brothers.

Although Clint didn't really know the Respits, he knew their type well enough. They were just like all the other thick-skulled men who thought that they could push their way through life without anyone ever pushing back. For some reason, those kind thought they were invincible. Instead they were just ignorant. Ignorant and mean.

Clint headed away from the sheriff's office and back toward Mil's. He could still see the look on the face of the man he'd seen standing next to Eclipse. He could see the stupid meanness in that one's eyes just as if he was staring into the face of a wild dog. He would get to Whiteoak's

wagon soon enough. First, however, he wanted to make sure
that there wasn't anything more pressing to be dealt with.

Eclipse waited for him outside Mil's, sloshing his snout
around in a half-full trough. Clint walked past the Darley
Arabian stallion and stepped up to the front door of the restaurant. He waited there for a second, listening for any sign
of trouble. He could hear nothing besides a few casual conversations and the clink of silverware on plates, but there
was something that made him uneasy. Thinking about the
look on that man's face put Clint on edge. It wasn't so much
his nerves, but a wariness he'd developed over years of dealing with violent men.

He pushed open the door and walked inside. Almost immediately, he spotted the man sulking at a table by himself
toward the back of the restaurant. Before he could make his
way over there, he saw someone approaching out of the corner of his eye.

"You must be starving by now," Mandy said as she
stepped between two tables crowded with customers. "It's
kinda busy, but I saved you a spot."

"Who is that?" Clint asked as he pointed to the table in
back.

Mandy didn't even have to look to know who Clint was
talking about. "That's Lee Respit. He came in a while ago,
and hasn't said a word except to order that stew. He stinks
of opium. I've been trying my best to keep clear of him."

"I'm going to have a talk with him."

"What about your supper?"

"Keep it warm for me. This shouldn't take long."

Lee had begun staring at Clint the instant he'd walked
through the door. Now that Clint walked around the tables
heading in his direction, the look on Lee's face only turned
darker and more intense.

"What the hell do you want?" Lee snarled once Clint
pulled up a chair and sat down.

"Just to talk."

"Like you did to that lousy piece of shit sittin' in jail?"

Clint put on his poker face to make sure the other man
didn't sense too much of his surprise. "Not exactly. I didn't
have to give up my gun to take part in this conversation."

His hand drifted down below the table as Lee shifted in his seat. Clint's motion stopped the other man cold.

"My brother said you went straight to that jail cell before you even got yerself a room for the night. What's so damn special about that professor?"

"First of all," Clint said, "I don't appreciate being followed. And second, my business here is none of yours. Third, I want to hear about your brother."

"He saw you walk from here to the sheriff's—"

"Not that one," Clint said after making sure his hand was resting solidly on his gun. "The dead one."

The corner of Lee's eyes twitched like there was an angry tick caught beneath the skin. He sat forward as though he was about to lunge across the table, but caught himself before committing himself to an attack. "I told you not to touch him. Now if you can do that, that's all you need to know about Owen."

"Who's Smitty?"

That got another reaction out of Lee. One that was aimed not so much at Clint, but at the world in general. The other man bared his teeth, grimacing as if he'd just inhaled a lung full of swamp gas. "If'n you even know to ask that question, you know goddamn well who he is." Another breath. Another bitter exhale. "He's the bastard that went to that medicine man so's he could buy his luck out of a bottle."

If he would have heard that statement yesterday, Clint would have laughed. Today, the words didn't sound quite so ridiculous.

"That professor gave him somethin' that made him kill my brother," Lee continued. "It's the only way that old man could've outdrawn Owen. It's the only way."

Suddenly, something changed in Lee's eyes. Clint could see it as though a cloud passed over the man's face. It seemed that whatever drug Lee had taken had been wearing off, but when his eyes glazed over and his scowl turned into a full-fledged expression of rage, every instinct in Clint's head told him that something had snapped inside Lee Respit. And for a moment, Clint swore he could hear it break.

"You know what I think?" Lee hissed as he pushed away

from the table. "I think you're tryin' to get rid of me before I catch up with that old man."

Clint matched the other man's movements, and they both stood up so fast that their chairs flew backward and toppled onto the floor.

"Just settle down now," Clint warned. His hand was near his gun, but he still hadn't drawn. "I'm just here to talk. I don't even know who this Smitty is. That's why·I asked."

Even though Clint was trying to keep his voice calm and soothing, Lee still reacted as if he was being directly challenged. He took a few steps back, warily scanning the room like a caged animal.

"I'm sick of hearin' that man's name," Lee said. "Sick of knowin' that he's out walking around while my brother's lyin' dead in the street."

As those words drifted about in the room, Clint could hear people all around him scooting their chairs back and getting ready to run for the door. A couple of the women in the restaurant were beginning to cry. From the corner of his eye, Clint could see Mandy standing still as a statue not five feet from his side.

There were too many people in here.

If guns started going off, one of these folks would catch a bullet just for being in the wrong place at the wrong time. Clint could tell by the way Lee was swaying from side to side that he was fighting to keep from falling over. The look in his eyes was one of nervous anger. Lee wouldn't fall over . . . not unless he was knocked over . . . and not before he tried to do as much damage as he could. Clint knew the man would have absolutely no regard for any of the innocent people sitting and standing by.

"To hell with all of ya!" Lee screamed as his hand went for the gun at his side.

Cursing under his breath, Clint committed himself to the only choice left open to him and threw himself in front of Lee's gun.

TEN

Clint leapt across the table with both hands outstretched, sending plates and half-full glasses crashing to the floor. Lee's eyes widened with surprise as he did his best to jerk the gun from his holster and take a shot from the hip.

But Lee wasn't nearly fast enough, and got the revolver only halfway out of its leather before Clint's hands grabbed hold of his arm. Lee let go of his gun so he could try to contend with the oncoming attacker, letting the pistol slide from his hands and snag on the edge of his holster, where it balanced and got ready to fall.

Using his momentum as his main weapon, Clint grabbed onto Lee's gun arm and twisted the man's elbow precisely the way nobody's arm is supposed to bend. He saw everything happen as though time itself had slowed down. The table wobbled beneath his weight as his body slid across. People on either side of him began to scatter and back away. But most importantly, he saw that the barrel of Lee's gun was caught inside the holster, its trigger guard caught along the upper edge. When Clint's shoulder plowed into Lee's chest, it was more than enough to send the gun toppling down, spinning end-over-end on its way to the floor.

It was then Clint also noticed that Lee had managed to cock the hammer back before getting tackled.

When the gun hit the floor, the impact was enough to set

it off, firing a single shot that blasted through the small restaurant and sent everybody but Clint and Lee stampeding for
the door. The bullet took a bite from the side of the table,
whipping past Clint's head before burying itself into the ceiling.

For a few seconds, all Clint could hear was the ringing in
his ears. As his world turned into a jumble of overturning
tables, flailing limbs, and oncoming fists, Clint let go of
Lee's arm so that he could steady himself before he slid off
the table completely.

As soon as he twisted his body around so that he was lying
across the table on his stomach, Clint pitched himself backward to get his feet back under him and dodge the fist that
was coming straight toward his face. He landed solidly with
both boots on the floor, continuing the motion as he ducked
just below Lee's punch.

Clint could see that Lee was trying to say something, but
he still couldn't make out much else besides the lingering
echo from the gunshot. Rather than swing at Lee's face with
a punch of his own, Clint grabbed hold of the wobbling table
with both hands and threw the edge sharply up, overturning
it so that it dropped onto Lee's legs.

Lee tried to step back, but was too late to keep his toes
from being smashed by the round table. His head arched back
as a howl of pain escaped his lips, and he swung wildly over
the tabletop, just barely managing to clip Clint across the
jaw.

Thinking that the other man was going to swing with the
left hand, which was closer, Clint bobbed in the wrong direction, all but walking into Lee's right fist as it came around
with a vicious haymaker. Clint's hearing was just starting to
come back when he felt the impact on his chin. His jaw
snapped to the side at a painful angle and the sound of wet
gristle cracking filled his ears. Bolts of pain shot through his
entire face, reaching down to his guts and twisting them sick-
eningly.

A nasty smile slid onto Lee's face and his shoulders shook
with laughter, leaving him wide open for Clint's right-hand
uppercut. When his fist pounded into Lee's midsection, Clint
knew he'd struck better than he could have hoped. The other

man's body seemed to crumple around Clint's fist, and a rush of foul-smelling air was pushed from his lungs.

For a second, Clint thought he'd put the man down. But instead of falling over, Lee staggered back a few steps and began coughing up a mess of blood and spit from the back of his throat. Not wanting to waste the few seconds he'd bought, Clint shoved aside the table, which was rolling back and forth on the floor, and charged Lee with his shoulders angled low.

Lee spat out a red glob and his hands went reflexively for his holster. Finding it empty, he was too late to do much of anything before Clint was on him, driving his shoulder into the bottom of Lee's solar plexus.

Once Clint felt the impact of his tackle, he wrapped both arms around Lee's waist and kept shoving him back until they hit a wall strong enough to stop them. Suddenly, Lee's legs flew out in front of him, sweeping both of Clint's out from under him as well. Their backward motion had taken them into a cart full of dishes, and both men went toppling over the waist-high box in a tangle of arms and legs.

For a second, Clint felt dizzy as they both flew at an angle, up over the cart and toward the floor. Lee hit the ground first, and when Clint came sailing over to join him, he drove his shoulder into Lee's face with a resounding thud.

Both men lay still for the next moment, Clint in an awkward heap on top of Lee. Then Clint rolled to the side and got to his knees, his fist balled up and ready to put Lee down for the count. That turned out to be unnecessary, however, since Lee's eyes were rolled back in his skull and his hands twitched as though they were still trying to fight through unconsciousness.

Clint reached out to make sure the other man was all right. Although Lee looked as though he'd been dropped from a second-floor window, his breathing was steady and nothing appeared too badly damaged. Clint then got to his feet and reached a hand up to rub his swollen jaw.

"Are you all right?" said a dazed voice from behind him.

Clint wheeled around, the motion sending jabs of pain through his ribs and neck. Mandy stood huddled near the kitchen, clutching a large black skillet and wielding it like a

club. Besides himself, Lee, and the waitress, Clint couldn't
see anyone else inside the restaurant. He surveyed the main
dining area and found a smaller mess than he'd been expecting.

There were the overturned table and chairs, along with the
broken cart sitting in the middle of a pool of broken dishes,
which left the rest of the room relatively unscathed. Compared to the way he felt, Clint thought the place should have
looked a lot worse. He felt better when he looked back down
at Lee.

"Did you kill him?" Mandy asked as she inched closer
toward the prone figure with her skillet raised up over her
head.

"He'll be all right," Clint said. He could tell his jaw wasn't
broken, but that didn't ease any of the pain he felt when he
talked. He started to walk back toward the upturned table to
get Lee's gun, then felt something warm and wet on his hip.
When he took another step, fiery pain shot from that spot to
rake down his entire leg.

Clint's hand went automatically for that hip, and came
away covered in blood. Protruding from his leg was a shard
of broken plate that must have been wedged into him when
he'd landed on the floor.

"Oh, my God," Mandy said. Dropping the skillet, she
rushed over to Clint's side and pulled a towel from her apron.
She pressed it to his hip and slid underneath one of his arms
to support him.

Wincing, Clint said, "Just feels like a flesh wound."

"All the same, you're coming with me. I can patch you
up and it'll be quicker than trying to find the doctor. I live
right across the street."

"Hold it," Clint said as he leaned down to retrieve Lee's
gun. After tucking the pistol in his belt on the opposite side
of his own gun, Clint clamped his hand over the towel on
his hip and walked on his own toward the door.

ELEVEN

They had just made it to the opposite side of the street when Mandy began tugging on Clint's shirt.

"Better hold up a second," she said. "Looks like we've got someone that wants to talk to us."

Clint turned slowly around to see Sheriff Kenrick hurrying toward him. He waited for the lawman to get a little closer before speaking. "He's in there," Clint said while pointing over at Mil's.

"It was Lee," Mandy added. "I saw the whole thing, and Lee just started like he was gonna pull his gun when Clint took him down."

The sheriff looked ready to either arrest Clint or run for the restaurant. "Someone said they heard gunshots."

Clint gave a quick rundown of what happened, trying to ignore the pain in his jaw that accompanied every single word. He finished off the account by handing over Lee's gun. "You should be able to get him easy enough," Clint said. "If you need me, I'll be across the street."

Mandy took Clint's arm and led him toward a squat, two-story building directly across from Mil's. "He'll be in my place, Sheriff. I'll tend to him and make sure he gets some rest. I owe him that much."

Kenrick seemed satisfied with the explanation he'd gotten. "If I didn't know Lee so well, I'd want you to come back

down to my office. But as it is, I'll ask you to not leave town
right away . . . just in case."

"Don't worry," Clint said. "I'm not in the mood for running anywhere right now."

Mandy's home was on the second floor of a two-story house.
The place was a lot nicer than the shoddy exterior of the
building, and even seemed a bit too nice to belong to a simple waitress. Every window had lace curtains, and the solid
oak furniture was well polished. Most of the floor was covered with a large woven rug.

Besides a small couch, there was a carved coffee table in
the living room area, and a large bookshelf took up one wall.
A door in the back of the room was closed. The entire place
slowly came to light as Mandy went around the room and
turned up a few lanterns scattered on various tables or hanging from the occasional hook.

"This is a nice place," Clint said as he dropped himself
down onto the couch.

Mandy shrugged, and used her apron to wipe oil from the
lanterns off her hands. "My mother used to own a lot of the
businesses in town. She left me this place along with enough
to keep me going. Before you ask, I work at the restaurant
because I couldn't bear sitting up in here doing nothing all
day."

"Can't say as I blame you. No matter how nice a place is,
I can't seem to stay put for too long myself."

Mandy reached down and took the bloody rag from Clint's
hand. After tossing it into a washbasin, she replaced it with
a soft towel from a pile next to a cedar chest. "I've heard all
about you." Blushing, she cast her eyes downward while
pressing the towel to Clint's hip. "Well, I heard the stories
anyway."

The sting from the jagged wound was already beginning
to fade, and Clint knew that the shard couldn't have given
him much more than a bad scratch. "Well, be careful about
what stories you listen to. Most of them are likely made up.
I've heard a lot of them myself, and believe me, nobody
could do half the things I've heard credited to me."

Mandy's touch was firm, yet gentle, as she pressed the rag

against Clint's side, being careful not to push too hard. "I don't know," she said softly. "Even half of those things are pretty impressive. Watching you back there, seeing how you fought Lee without even minding the gun he had . . . it was really exciting."

When she removed the towel, it came back with just a thin streak of red. "Bleeding's almost stopped. But just to be safe . . ." Her hands drifted up to Clint's gunbelt and started working on the buckle.

"Mandy . . . you don't have to—"

"I know, Clint." Setting the gunbelt aside, she started in on the buttons of his shirt as well as the fastenings on his pants. "I know I don't have to, but I want to. Besides," she said while peeling the shirt from his body, "we need to get some air on these cuts and bruises of yours."

Although Clint's body ached from where he'd smashed into tables, chairs, floorboards, and fists, the discomfort he felt quickly faded away as Mandy's hands massaged his body and delicately worked him out of his clothes. She ran her hands down along his sides, just barely touching him with the tips of her fingers. She lingered over the spots that were turning black and blue before moving her hands down to help him out of his clothes.

Once he was naked, she took the towel and cleaned off the blood from his hip. After getting up to soak the towel in cool water, she pressed the cloth to his wound and leaned in to kiss him gently on the lips. His body responded to the combination of cool from the cloth and hot from her mouth. When he reached up to pull her closer, Mandy moved away and got to her feet.

"Come on," she said while taking his hand. "I've got some bandages in the other room. You can rest easier in there."

She led him to the door at the back of the room, which opened onto a small but comfortable bedroom. There was a cabinet with another washbasin, as well as a large wardrobe sitting next to a thin rectangular window. Most of the space was taken up by a large four-poster bed that was covered with a hand-stitched down comforter.

Clint stepped inside the room and sat down on the edge of the bed. Mandy poked about in a cabinet, and came out with an old apron similar to the one she was wearing.

"I don't have any bandages after all," she said. "But this should do for a little cut like that." She then began to tear the apron into narrow strips. Once she had three or four of them, she knelt down in front of Clint and began wrapping them around his lower hip and upper thigh.

She moved her hands slowly over the wound, being careful not to wrap the material too tightly. Once she'd tied it off, Mandy touched Clint's thigh, exploring his muscles as her lips explored his chest.

For the next few moments, all the pain in Clint's body was forgotten. He suddenly didn't care about his nearly broken jaw or the beating the rest of him had taken. He didn't even care about Henry Whiteoak for the time being.

All that concerned him was the beautiful woman who was now cupping his hardening penis in her hand. She rubbed his shaft lovingly while flicking her tongue over his nipples and then licking up along his neck. He could feel her hot breath on his skin, and by the time she was pressing her mouth over his, Clint's hands were busy tearing at her clothes.

A wicked little smile played across Mandy's face as she moved onto the bed and allowed herself to be undressed.

TWELVE

Mandy's body was slim and smooth beneath the blue cotton dress. Her dark hair spilled over her shoulders and came to a gentle curl right above her firm, pert breasts. Clint pressed her closer to him so he could taste her flesh. Holding her tightly against his body, he ran his tongue over her lips and then began nibbling at the base of her neck.

She wrapped her arms around him then, breathing heavily into his ear, letting out little moans when his teeth bit lightly into her skin. Clint's hands moved up over her hips, along her sides, and onto her breasts. They were supple and warm to the touch, and she squealed in delight when he lightly pinched her nipples.

"Mmmm, Clint," she whispered. "I hope this helps you feel better."

Clint took her up in his arms and positioned her so that she was lying on her stomach with her head resting on one of the bed's fluffy pillows. "Why don't you tell me?" he said as he pressed himself on top of her. His hard shaft slid down the curve of her tight, rounded buttocks and then pushed between her legs. "How do I feel?"

Mandy reached out to grab the top of the mattress while turning her head to look at him over her shoulder. "That feels good," she said while pulling herself up onto her knees facing away from him.

47

He then reached around to cup her breasts. The nipples were small and hard, and when Clint moved his hands over them, she closed her eyes and leaned her head back. Clint moved his hands down the front of her body. Her stomach was tight and muscled, moving in and out with every one of her quick, shallow breaths. Her hips were slender and lean, but tapered to an elegant curve. He then let his hands drift down to her thighs, which were taut and sinewy with well-toned muscle.

Mandy smiled widely with her eyes still closed as she reached behind her to run her fingers through Clint's hair. When his hands slid between her legs, she arched her back and spread her legs a little more. She moaned softly as his fingers slid down her moist folds before slipping inside her tight opening.

Clint savored the feel of her hot dampness as he moved his fingers in and out of her, gently exploring her creamy depths. As soon as he moved his hands, she twisted around to face him, pressing her groin hard against his rigid pole.

Still smiling, she held his wrists and guided his hands up to her mouth. Once there, she slowly extended her pink little tongue and licked her own juices from Clint's fingers.

Not wanting to wait another instant, Clint reached down and cupped Mandy's bottom, lifting her up and setting her back down again so that she was sitting up against the head-board. He leaned down to kiss her deeply on the mouth. When his tongue moved over hers, he could taste her sex mingled in with the sweetness of her lips, and wanting more, he kissed her even harder.

"What do I taste like?" she whispered in his ear.

Clint moved his body down along hers, enjoying the feel of her flesh rubbing against him. "I couldn't say for sure. Guess that means I'll have to try a little more."

He then slid down the length of the bed until he was kneeling on the floor. After pulling Mandy down so that her legs dangled over the side, Clint put his face between her legs and ran his tongue over her moist, glistening lips. Her entire body shuddered as he tasted her, and soon her legs were wrapped around his head, gripping him tightly.

Her juices ran down Clint's face, making it easier for him

to slide his face up and down ... side to side ... and eventually in little circles. Mandy's entire body squirmed in ecstasy until she was begging for more.

"Oh, Clint ... please put your tongue in me. Do it now."

He let her ask a few more times before finally holding her open with two fingers and burying his tongue deep inside her. Now Mandy began to buck against his face, and she sat up to grab hold of his hair, pulling him deeper between her legs. When her screams got louder, she let her body drop back onto the bed and pushed her hips out as pleasure washed over her body from head to toe.

"My whole body's on fire," she moaned. "But I need more."

Clint didn't say a word. Instead, he laid her down and climbed on top of her squirming form. Breathing heavily with anticipation, Mandy spread herself open wide and gritted her teeth as Clint impaled her with his stiff cock. They both cried out as he slid himself all the way inside and held it there for a few seconds.

Looking down at her, Clint took in the sight of her sweaty body. Her nipples were so hard they left little shadows by the dim lantern light. She reached up to play with them, squeezing them as he began pumping between her thighs.

With her hands stretched over her head, Mandy arched her back and tensed every muscle in her body. Clint could feel her legs trembling around him, and could see the waves of passion sweeping through her. She clenched around him and her screams became louder, until finally she relaxed her muscles and grabbed hold of Clint's arms.

She disentangled from him and pushed him over onto his back. After Clint was lying diagonally across the bed, she climbed on top of him and rubbed her body against his in a slow, serpentine dance. Straddling his hips, Mandy reached down to stroke Clint's rod. Her hands slid down its length until she finally maneuvered it between her legs.

Clint let out a slow moan as she lowered herself onto him, impaling herself on his hard cock. Reaching for her hips, he grabbed hold of her and guided her pace as she rode on top of him. He used his thumbs to rub the sensitive nub of flesh over her opening, causing her to lean back and cry out with delight.

Her pert breasts shook as her body rose and fell. Her lips parted as though she was too tired to make any more noise. Moving her hands behind her body, Mandy held on to Clint's legs while pumping her hips back and forth. Clint cupped her firm little rump with both hands, keeping her steady as he thrust up inside her.

When he climaxed, Clint clenched his eyes shut so tightly that little red dots appeared in front of him. The blood pumped through his body so quickly that the room felt as though it had started to spin. The release felt so good that he didn't even know he was moaning until he'd run out of breath.

When he tried to pull out of her, Mandy leaned forward and clenched her legs around him tighter. "Not yet," she pleaded. "Please, not yet."

Seeing her face contorted with such intense pleasure, Clint could feel his cock getting hard again inside her. Her body tightened around him, making him even stiffer. He only needed to pound inside her a few more times before Mandy was raking her fingernails down Clint's chest and whipping her hair from side to side.

Her body collapsed on top of Clint's, and it seemed to take all of Mandy's strength to roll onto the mattress beside him. Exhausted, they fell asleep in each other's arms. Neither one knew what time it was when they woke up, but in the dead of night, her home was once again filled with their cries.

THIRTEEN

The next morning, Clint woke up to find Mandy still curled up next to him. He had a lot of things to do and wanted to get an early start, so he'd managed to wake up just after dawn. Sounds of activity from the street came drifting through the window, mainly coming from the restaurant directly across from the house. When he went to the window, Clint took in a deep lungful of air, and immediately caught the scent of bacon frying.

Within ten minutes, he was dressed and ready to go. After gently waking Mandy, he asked her if she wanted to join him for breakfast. Apparently she liked her job, but not enough to go to the restaurant when she wasn't scheduled to wait on tables. That was fine with Clint, who went over to have a delicious meal of fresh biscuits, coffee, eggs, and bacon at a table by himself, served by another, older, less comely waitress.

As soon as he was finished, he got up to pay his bill and leave. Before he could make it to the door, however, he heard a voice coming from the kitchen area.

"Mister, wait a second."

Turning, Clint saw the portly Indian cook standing in the kitchen door, wiping his hands on a towel that was resting on his shoulder. After he saw that he'd gotten Clint's attention, the cook motioned for him to wait and said something

to someone else in the other room. After a few words and a
nod of his head, the cook made his way from the kitchen
and approached Clint.

"A minute of your time, if it's convenient?" the cook re-
quested.

"No problem," Clint said. "What's on your mind?"

The cook nodded toward the front door and began walking
in that direction. Clint followed, and found the Indian standing outside with a bag of tobacco and rolling paper in hand.
He sprinkled a small amount of tobacco onto the paper and
began twisting it with practiced hands.

The cook shrugged and struck a match. "Owners don't like
me doing it in the kitchen," he said while touching the flame
to the end of his cigarette. "Thought you might want to know
what happened to that man you were fighting last night." He
took a long pull of smoke into his lungs and let it out in an
easy breath.

Nodding, Clint said, "It would save me a trip to the
sheriff's office."

The cook laughed at that. "It sure would. Sheriff Kenrick
came in, yelled at Lee, and made a real show of it." He took
another drag. "But that's all it was. A show."

"Did Lee fight much when he was brought in?"

"Nope. Not at all. 'Cause he never came within a hundred
feet of that jail."

Clint felt his stomach tighten into a knot. If there was one
thing that bothered him more than a crooked lawman, he
couldn't think of it. He'd known so many men who sacrificed
everything and laid down their lives to uphold the law, and
when men tarnished the badges they wore by using them for
their own profit, it took away from the others who fought
and died to do their jobs the right way. Another thing that
was creeping up on the edge of Clint's mind was the notion
that Henry Whiteoak might just be telling the truth.

"I heard Mandy talking about you," the cook said. "I recognized your name. So I guess you've been around enough
to know what kind of man Kenrick is, judging by what he
does."

"I'm not much of a judge."

The cigarette in the cook's mouth waggled up and down

as another chuckle shook his shoulders. "The judge is a whole other story."

"You seem to know a lot about this town's politics for spending your days inside a kitchen. Why are you so interested in all of this? And why pull me aside to tell me about it?"

Now the Indian's face lost all traces of humor. When he took another puff of his cigarette, it seemed as if he wanted to calm his nerves rather than satisfy a simple craving. "I've heard a lot about you, Mr. Adams. Friends of mine from Dodge City and Salt Lake tell me that you listen to people when they need help. That you fight when you're needed and always seem to choose the right side."

Clint shrugged slightly and shook his head. "It's not as noble as it sounds, but I guess you could say that I don't like to stand by and watch things happen that shouldn't."

"There's trouble brewing here. Unless someone steps in, two men are gonna die. People around here are either too scared or just plain don't care about it, but I don't find it so easy to turn my back."

Clint looked around the street and watched as people strolled by, purposely turning their faces away from the cook. The ones that did allow themselves to look at the Indian were obviously doing so with contempt. It wasn't anything so strong as hatred that Clint felt directed toward the other man. It was more like forced tolerance. He'd seen it in plenty of people who made it a habit to look down at others, whether it be blacks, Indians, Mexicans, or Chinese.

"By the way," Clint said, "I never caught your name."

The statement seemed to surprise the cook more than anything else. Reluctantly, he held out his hand and looked directly into Clint's eyes. "My name's Sam."

After shaking Sam's hand, Clint turned and looked down the street toward the body, which was still lying there. "So, I guess it's a pretty safe guess that one of these men in danger is this Smitty fellow who shot Lee's brother."

"That's right."

The strangest thing about that rotting corpse wasn't so much that it was on display in the middle of a road, but that the people seemed to walk around it as though Owen had every right to lie down and decompose in front of God and everybody. Even now, with carriages making their way from one end of town to another, drivers simply steered around the thing, ignoring the protests of their horses when the animals caught its foul stench. People walked as fast as they could to go by the corpse, not stopping until they were half a block away from it.

"Am I the only one that thinks it's strange that Lee wants his brother to sit out there instead of giving him a proper burial?" Clint asked.

"No. You're just the only one who doesn't mind saying it out loud." The cigarette was almost burned down to Sam's fingers, but rather than stub it out, the Indian put it to his lips and savored the last wisp of smoke before feeling the heat. "Lee's not crazy like everyone thinks."

Once the cigarette was nothing more than a scrap of lit paper, Sam flicked it to the ground. "Y' see that building there?" he asked while pointing toward the spot where Owen was still lying.

Clint looked past the corpse and saw a telegraph office, a boarded-up storefront, and what looked like a small saloon.

"The one in the middle," Sam said. "The one that looks just as dead as Owen."

"Yeah. I see it."

"Well, you're the only one."

At first, Clint thought that the cook had been smoking something besides tobacco. But then he took a moment to watch the people as they walked around the body. They turned their faces away and quickened their steps, shuffling past the storefront as though it didn't even exist. Not that there was much to look at besides a tightly shut door and dirty windows, but there wasn't even so much as a glance aimed at that place, or the others on either side of it for that matter.

"So?" Clint asked. "What are they supposed to be looking at?"

"Maybe you should ask the other man that's in danger of getting his life cut short. I heard him talking to Lee at the restaurant, and they both seemed pretty interested in that old place. So interested that Lee nearly put a bullet in the fella's head right there at his favorite table."

"I don't suppose you know who that man is?" Clint asked, even though he had the sinking feeling that he already knew who it was.

"You may not know his name, but he's cooling his heels in jail right now, which is right where Lee wants him."

A heavy sigh worked its way up from Clint's gut and pushed itself out of his mouth. It didn't feel as bad as when he first knew that Whiteoak was in town, but it was close.

"That one's in enough trouble," Sam continued. "But it ain't enough to get him killed. I've met him before. The professor may be full of shit, but his heart's in the right place."

That snapped Clint back to attention. "I've met him too. And the last thing I thought I'd ever hear him get accused of is having a good heart. Forgery, cheating at cards, swindling, fast-talking, maybe even robbery, but not much else besides that."

"You obviously remember Henry," Sam said. "But I just hope you're as impartial as you say. Anyway, I've got to get back inside. Thanks for hearing me out."

Clint watched the Indian step back inside Mil's, and took a moment to think about what Sam had said. There was a lot to chew on, and most of it seemed to revolve around a dead man rotting in the street and a con man rotting in jail.

He knew he might hate himself for it later, but Clint decided to see if there was anything behind the favorable comments Sam had made about the professor.

"Great," he mumbled to himself. "Maybe I should buy a bottle of miracle tonic while I'm at it."

FOURTEEN

Clint had taken Eclipse to the livery during the night after he'd gotten settled in at Mandy's. The place was nothing special. In fact, he wouldn't have even noticed it if not for the colorful painted wagon stored in one of the corners of a large corral.

Now Clint walked into the livery as though he was just checking up on Eclipse. The Darley Arabian nodded its head up and down when it saw Clint enter the stable. He patted the stallion's muzzle and fussed with Eclipse's shoe until the liveryman found something else better to do than watch him.

Clint then got up and walked straight out the back of the stable and into the corral out back. There were a few carts and a pair of flatbed wagons. Whiteoak's was by itself in a far corner, sitting like an abandoned circus tent. Clint remembered that the wagon had looked garish before, but when he saw it now parked next to the other wagons, the thing looked positively hideous.

The steel rims of the wheels were chipped, and had obviously been pounded into shape several times. The body was made of sturdy, if slightly warped, cedar, which had been built to survive the elements. Along the bottom of the cart was a row of small rectangular drawers, each one with its own brass-framed keyhole. The cover was thick canvas and painted with big, bold letters proclaiming the various miracles contained within. Everything had its price, which was stenciled in smaller letters along the bottom of the tarp.

Clint circled around the wagon, running his hand along knots in the wood as well as a good amount of bullet holes both old and new. Although the paint was fresher, it was the same rig that he remembered from when he'd met Whiteoak years ago. He walked around so that the wagon was between him and the stable before kneeling down and reaching his hand beneath the front axle.

Sure enough, he quickly found a small leather pouch nailed to the wood just behind the right wheel. It took a few tries, but finally Clint managed to tear the sack away from the axle. It was a little pouch, which just fit into the palm of his hand. When he began tugging it open, the pouch jingled like a woman's coin purse.

Since it was tied shut with a tangle of tight little knots, Clint had to poke his finger through a rip in the leather he'd made when pulling it from the bottom of the wagon. The leather gave easily enough, after having been weakened by all the puddles it had splashed through over the years of travel.

Clint held his hand beneath the rip on the leather and shook the pouch. Two keys fell into his palm. One was smaller than his fingernail, and the other was more of a normal size and looked like it might fit into a safe or a strongbox.

First, Clint went to the front of the wagon. Because it was facing away from the stables, he was able to climb up into the driver's seat without worrying too much about attracting attention from the liveryman. He did so, and immediately noticed how well maintained the wagon truly was.

Despite having the appearance of a garishly colored mess of warped timber, the supports beneath the seat bent silently beneath Clint's weight as if they were brand-new. The seat itself was worn just enough to be comfortable, and it took a good couple of minutes for him to find the iron box hidden underneath even though he'd been told where to look. A piece of wood fit perfectly over a small square compartment, covering it so that it blended in flawlessly right down to the grain. A knothole just big enough to get a fingernail under was the only thing allowing Clint to pry up the cover, but once he did, it popped up to reveal a dull gray iron strongbox.

Clint's back was beginning to cramp up after spending the last few minutes hunched over to look between his legs at the wagon's floor. He knew the liveryman would probably be looking for him, so he grabbed hold of the box, dug it out of the compartment, and held it beneath his arm.

As he was climbing down, he spotted another little compartment where the professor kept a small .32-caliber pistol squirreled away between the driver's seat and brake lever. It wasn't the most original spot to keep a gun, but the way it was constructed, even someone looking for a hideaway weapon would more than likely overlook it. He could feel the need to hurry chewing at his gut. On his way around the wagon, Clint went to the drawer along the side that Whiteoak had told him about. The second key fit perfectly into the miniature hole and when he twisted it, the small drawer nearly popped into his hand.

Inside was another bundle, this one about the size of a flat bag of marbles. Without even looking at what it was, Clint grabbed the bundle and shoved it into his pocket. He then hurried back into the stables, just in time for the liveryman to stick his head through the door at the other end.

A scrawny man wearing dirty coveralls, the liveryman looked as though he smelled twice as bad as the animals he took care of. "Everything all right, mister?" the man asked through a mouthful of crooked, browning teeth.

"Just seeing if you had a different kind of feed," Clint said while pretending to nose around in a corner. "I'd prefer it if you went easy on the greens."

The liveryman wiped his hands on his chest, leaving dark wet smears along the front of his coveralls. "I'll take care of it fer ya."

Clint put on a look of concern, and then nodded as he walked past Eclipse's stall. "Much obliged," he said after giving the stallion a scratch behind its ears.

The strongbox fit snugly beneath Clint's arm. He held it there as though it wasn't anything out of the ordinary. The liveryman seemed unconcerned by anything with less than four legs, and stepped aside to let Clint pass.

He walked to the first saloon he could find on his way to the sheriff's office. It was a small room that smelled of sweat and beer. The bar itself was no bigger than a closet door laid on its side. At this time of the day, there were only a few drunks who looked as though they only took their faces up off the bar when they had to dump their last three drinks in the outhouse. Then again, Clint thought as he took another whiff of the air in the place, maybe they didn't even get up for that.

The first thing he did was fit the smallest of Whiteoak's keys into the hole of the strongbox so he could open it up and take a look inside. The next thing he did was order a drink because he suddenly felt as though he needed one.

FIFTEEN

"I'll be damned," Clint whispered as he opened the book-sized strongbox.

Inside was a wad of cash that might have been enough to buy Whiteoak's freedom even if he'd tried to kill someone. The first layer of bills would have gotten him out of Kenrick's jail faster than it would have taken the sheriff to turn the key. What surprised Clint more than anything else was the fact that Henry Whiteoak had obviously been telling the truth about his situation.

Clint was a long way from buying into the entire story, but any con man worth his salt would have gotten as far away from the law as humanly possible if he'd had the means. Well, Whiteoak had the means. Clint was looking at it. There was so much stuffed inside the box that he didn't feel comfortable taking it out in a public place to count it all. Instead, he discreetly shut the lid and locked it tight before setting it on the floor and putting his boot on top of it just to be sure.

The next thing he wanted to do was open the small pouch that he'd found in one of the locked drawers of Whiteoak's wagon. He dug around in his pocket and pulled out what felt like a bundle of papers tightly wrapped in cloth. The package was held together with a piece of twine wrapped around it all so tightly that Clint needed to cut it with his pocketknife in order to look inside.

The cloth fell away to reveal a set of deeds folded up like a bunch of letters. He was no prospector, but Clint knew legal documents when he saw them, and if these weren't such papers, they were excellent forgeries. The deeds were mainly for properties in California and Colorado, but there were a few in Wyoming as well as one at the bottom of the pile for a place in Utah.

Chester, Utah, to be exact.

Clint glanced through the document and found that it was not for a mine, but for a lot in the middle of town. More specifically, the deed seemed to emphasize the rights to anything found "on, around, or within the property grounds."

While Clint wasn't familiar with exactly where the address of this property was, he had a pretty good guess where to start looking even before he asked for any local's help. Based on his conversation with Sam, he was beginning to get a better picture of what was going on. It was a picture that was still slightly out of focus and downright foggy around the edges, but it was better than what he'd had before.

After folding the documents and wrapping them back up, Clint ordered a beer and drank less than half of it. The brew was about as good as could be expected from such a hole of a saloon, but even the pungent flavor wasn't enough to truly catch Clint's attention. He was too busy thinking about what he'd heard, seen, and more importantly, read.

If those deeds were genuine, then they were worth a hell of a lot of money. Just the mines in California and Colorado alone would be worth a pretty penny to any prospector with high hopes. And if a quarter of them actually panned out, the man with those deeds in hand could wind up sitting on top of a small fortune. It was also Clint's experience that betting on a crooked game of faro was usually a wiser gamble than buying into a mine. But that didn't mean that there weren't plenty of people out there willing to kill for their chance at the big payoff.

Henry Whiteoak was one of those men. And Clint was beginning to get the idea that Lee Respit was one as well.

●   ●   ●

The gun felt cold and heavy in Lee's hand. He pressed it up against his forehead to try to ease the raging thunderstorm that was going on in there as the opium and alcohol burned their way through his system. His head was pounding, and the rest of him felt as though it had been kicked in by a mule. When he opened his eyes, the sunlight burned through to the back of his skull. The floor began tilting as if it was trying to catch up with the spinning walls.

"You don't look so good," Nickolas Respit said.

Lee fought back the urge to hit his brother, but decided it was the only bit of pleasure he might get anytime soon. When the back of his fist smashed into the younger man's jaw, Lee felt a little better . . . if only for a few seconds.

"Owww," Nickolas whined. "What'd you do that for?"

"That's for talkin' so damn loud! Don't your own head feel like it's about to split open?"

"No, but I wasn't the one that had to go out drinkin' on top of everything else."

"Then that was my mistake, wasn't it?" Waiting until Nickolas leaned in a little closer, Lee nailed him across the other side of his jaw. "And that was for rubbin' my face in it. Now what the hell are you doin' here anyways?"

Nickolas wheeled around so that his back was to his brother, and both hands went up to his bloody mouth. His lip had been split open in two places, but he knew better than to let on about his pain. Lee never liked to hear someone else complain. It only made the beatings worse. He was a lot like Pa in that respect.

"I thought you'd want to know about that fella that knocked you out last night," Nickolas said after he'd stepped out of arm's reach.

Lee tried to lunge forward, but stopped when he felt his body starting to head straight for the floor. Instead, he steadied himself with a hand against the back of a chair and dropped back down onto his bed. They were in Lee's bedroom in the Respit home on the edge of town. It wasn't a big place, especially considering that it had contained a family of eight within its three rooms. All the rest of the land went to the ranch that had long ago gone to seed.

Growing up inside the house had been an experience of

constantly dodging blows and bodies as people rattled around in what was essentially a kitchen and two closets with cots packed inside them. The bigger of the two closet-sized rooms had belonged to Ma and Pa, who couldn't even get dressed in there at the same time. Lee and his three brothers and two sisters had taken turns sleeping in the kitchen. Now that it was down to just the two brothers, the house was a bit roomier, although far from comfortable.

"I only lost because of the damn smoke and liquor," Lee said as he lowered his head to a sack half full of feathers that passed for a pillow and hung his feet over the end of the cot. "If it'd been a fair fight, I would've broken that stranger's neck with my bare hands."

"Just so long as you don't try to draw down on him."

Lee glared across the room at his younger brother, and watched as the grown man cowered in the doorway like he was trying to hide from the boogeyman. "What the hell do you know about it anyway? You wasn't even there."

"Do you know who that stranger is?"

"I don't have ta know a goddamn thing about him. All I need—"

"He's Clint Adams."

The name sounded familiar to Lee. Of course he'd heard about The Gunsmith, but there was something else . . . like maybe he'd heard that name the previous night as well. The more he thought about it, the name made his hungover brain hurt even more. Lee scowled and tried to cover up the bad feeling creeping into his stomach. "How'd you hear about that? From one of them Chinese you associate with?"

"No. I heard it from the sheriff when I went to get him."

"Oh, so it was you that called the law?" Lee asked while pressing his fingertips to his throbbing temples. "Thanks a lot, little brother."

Nickolas ignored the dig. "It was either that or watch you get killed. Kenrick said that the Gunsmith was in town and was even talking to that professor who's locked up in jail."

"He ain't no professor," Lee snarled with a sudden viciousness that caused Nickolas to take another step out of the cramped room.

"Whatever he is, just watch your step around him, Lee."

Suddenly, the older Respit surged forward and nearly jumped to his feet. If he was in a normal-sized room, he probably would have fallen right back to the ground. But as it was, the walls were close enough to steady him. Even the ceiling was low enough to provide support for his wildly searching hands. Lee stood hunched over, filling the tiny room.

"Gunsmith or not . . . there ain't no man that's gonna come between me and twenty-five thousand dollars. I nearly took him down when I was dead drunk, so that means I can kill him whenever I want—after I sober up . . .

"And as for that son of a bitch Whiteoak . . . I'll hang him from the rafters of that goddamn jail cell even if I have to blow a hole through Kenrick and walk straight through it."

SIXTEEN

Clint was on his way back from a quick trip across town, where he'd managed to stash Whiteoak's strongbox and documents for safekeeping. As much as he hated leaving the valuables, he knew they were safer as long as they were away from him. Heading back to the sheriff's office, he caught sight of a familiar face across the street. Mandy waved excitedly from the sidewalk, nearly stepping in front of an oncoming stagecoach in her haste to run up to Clint's side. She was dressed in a simple brown dress that cinched her breasts in tightly, gathering them to be displayed perfectly by a low-cut collar. A belt around her waist brought out the shape of her slim, curving hips.

After the stage rumbled by, she lifted her skirts to her ankles and ran across the street. Clint couldn't help but notice the way her pert breasts trembled within her clothing and the smooth, light brown complexion of her skin. Finally, Mandy slowed her pace and began walking alongside him.

"I thought you'd still be at Mil's," she said between heavy breaths. "I went over there and Sam told me you'd already gone."

"I had some business to take care of." Taking hold of the top of her arm, Clint pulled her closer to let a white mare trot down the street without knocking her over.

"I thought you'd done your piece and left town," she said.

"I was beginning to plan some nasty things for you."

Clint pulled her even closer, even though there wasn't anything around to run her over. "And what about now?"

Her hair smelled faintly of honeysuckle and was pulled back with a black ribbon. Smiling widely, she said, "I've still got plans for you." She leaned in and kissed him gently on his upper lip. "They're still nasty, but not as painful," she added while flicking out her tongue so quickly that Clint could just barely feel its warm wetness touch his mouth.

A few of the people passing by gave them strange looks, but none of them looked surprised. Clint pulled away and began walking slowly down the street, holding her hand inside his. "Can you tell me where Number Three South Third Street is?" he asked, rattling off the local address that was on one of Whiteoak's deeds.

"Sure. Actually," she said while pulling him in another direction, "you can just about see it for yourself from here."

They came to an intersection near the edge of town not too far from Mil's. Once they were there, Mandy lifted a finger to indicate the end of the street occupied by the body of Owen Respit. "Number Three is right over there," she said. "It's the one behind . . ."

Clint had been ready to put money down on where the address was, but he wanted to check just to make sure. When he looked down the street, past the crumpled body, he could see exactly what he'd been expecting. Number Three was the boarded-up storefront right beside the telegraph office and behind the body.

"What do you need with that place?" Mandy asked. "There hasn't even been anyone using that old space for nearly a year now."

Clint shrugged. "Just something I heard in passing. They must have been talking about where to stay away from . . . with Owen and all."

"So where are you headed?"

"Actually, I was going back to talk to the sheriff about some things. Maybe see if I can be of any help with that professor he's got in custody."

A look drifted across Mandy's face that made her look as though she'd caught a whiff of something left behind by a skunk. "That professor don't deserve no help. He ain't nothing but a cheat who deserves whatever he's got coming to him."

"You sound like you're talking from experience." Clint turned away from the dead body and began walking in the direction of Sheriff Kenrick's office. The amount of people walking down Owen's street was down to a trickle. When he turned back toward Mil's, Clint felt as though he was standing on the line between two completely different towns.

Mandy hooked her arm through Clint's. "I've seen enough of his kind. They drift through town, preaching like they had God in a bottle, and then say whatever you want to hear so long as you've got enough money in your hand."

"I agree with you," Clint said. "But there must be some people in town who bought what the professor was selling."

"Oh, there's plenty of fools in this world. It's just too bad more of them don't learn from their mistakes."

They were walking past Mil's now, and Mandy took a look inside. The place had nearly emptied out, but the smells still hung in the air as if to lure in the occasional late riser. Clint could still taste the bacon on the back of his tongue.

"Does Whiteoak come through Chester very often?" he asked casually.

Mandy turned her face away from the restaurant and squinted in concentration. Her head turned toward her home across the street as though she'd written the answer to Clint's question on the back of her lace curtains. Finally, she said, "I believe he's been through here at least four times in the last year or so. I guess the pickin's must be pretty good for him to keep showing up. Either that, or he's been kicked out of every other respectable town in the county."

"That little saloon down by the telegraph office," Clint said. "Does he go there when he's in town?"

"Whenever I heard his voice blarin' out of that god-awful wagon of his, I just walked in the other direction. He could stick his face in the creek for a drink for all I care. I do know that he and Lee ate in Mil's plenty of times."

Clint's eyes snapped over toward Mandy, who was strolling easily beside him. "Lee and the professor got together when he was in town?"

"Sure seemed like it. Him and whatever cheap piece of trash that Lee was fucking at the time. They would all meet there at least once whenever that wagon pulled into the town limits."

Clint's head was swimming with bits and pieces of information gleaned from the conversation. Whiteoak coming through town to visit his investment sounded reasonable enough. And if he was talking to Lee about it . . . well, that could explain a lot of the troubles the professor had had since then. Actually, Clint realized that if he hadn't met Whiteoak before, he would already have begun to try to help the man rather than trying to find yet another way to prove his story.

They were less than half a block away from the sheriff's office when Mandy came to a sudden stop and put her hands on her hips. "Why do you care so much about that professor person anyway?" she asked.

"Just trying to soak up some of the local flavor," Clint said with a lopsided smile. "Doesn't a man have a right to be curious when he nearly gets shot his first night in town?"

Mandy's face softened and she ran her hands down Clint's shoulders. "Sorry. You're right. That liar just gets me riled up, is all. And I don't want to see you messing around with anyone else that might get you hurt. Not after I just found you."

Clint gave her a little kiss on the forehead and continued toward the sheriff's. "Forget it. How about you make it up to me tonight?"

She smiled and kept pace with him. "Sounds goods."

"Why don't you wait for me over at Mil's," Clint said once they were standing just outside Kenrick's door. "I'll meet you there around noon and we can have lunch."

Before she could answer, they were both shoved forward by a pair of rough hands. Clint started to turn around, but stopped short when he felt the cold metal of a gun barrel pressing into his spine.

SEVENTEEN

"Just walk inside slowly and don't try anything," said a ragged voice that hissed into Clint's ear. "Or I'll pull my trigger and burn you down before you can blink an eye."

Clint's muscles tensed in preparation for a quick turn. Then he thought about the woman at his side and abandoned his plan of action. Although he might have risked a fight if he was alone, he wasn't about to put Mandy's life in danger in the bargain. Instead, he moved his head to look reassuringly at Mandy and stepped inside. Nice and slow . . . just as he was instructed.

As soon as they entered the office, Clint looked around for any sight of the sheriff. While he couldn't see Kenrick, he could hear some activity coming from the jail cells in the next room. The gun in Clint's back jabbed painfully into him, prodding him along like a cow toward the slaughterhouse.

"There must be some mistake," Clint said.

Behind him, there was the sound of scuffling feet. Someone closed and locked the door, although the gun didn't move an inch from where it was digging into his backbone.

"Ain't no mistake," said the same voice, which was so close Clint could smell what the other man had had for breakfast. "You're the one that made the mistake when you decided to stick yer nose where it don't belong."

The only thing missing from Lee's voice was the tint of

opium and whiskey on his breath. It took a second for Clint
to place it without being yelled at from across a table, but
there wasn't much of a chance for him to forget about a man
who'd tried to kill him the night before.

"Mind if I have a seat, Respit, or are you going to shoot
me in the back?" Clint asked while raising his hands in the
air. "You might not have been much of a match last night,
but I figured you for a bigger man than this."

The steel pressing against Clint's back gave him a sharp
stabbing pain as Lee shoved him forward toward a chair in
front of the sheriff's desk. Clint caught himself before he
lost his balance, and turned to make sure Mandy was all
right. She looked more scared than hurt, and was already
lowering herself into a chair closer to the door.

Once he was turned around, Clint could see that Lee was
indeed the one holding the gun on him, while another
younger man had positioned himself in front of the door.
Clint watched as that second man gently asked Mandy if she
would please get closer to the desk. He was holding his gun
as though it was something alive and squirming in his hand.
Instinctively, Clint marked that one as the weak link.

Lee waited until Clint was in a chair before letting his
shoulders relax and his gun hand creep in closer to his hip.
"Y'know, most people take a friendly warning when they get
one," Lee rasped. "They steer clear from where they ain't
wanted and leave when they're asked. But not you, huh?"

"I guess you could call that a flaw in my character," Clint
said dryly.

"Well, you're about to have a flaw in that clean shirt of
yours in a second," Lee said while thumbing back the hammer of his pistol. "A big, bloody flaw that'll go all the way
through to the back."

Suddenly, a voice boomed from down the hall that led to
the jail cells. "Just cool down, Lee. Nobody's shooting any-
body until I say so."

Clint recognized the voice, but he had to look to be absolutely sure. Actually, he would have felt better if his hearing had been playing tricks on him rather than seeing the
truth play itself out right in front of him. Walking from the

door, holding a shotgun in one hand and the end of a rope in another, was Sheriff Kenrick.

"And how long are you fools gonna wait," the sheriff said, "before someone takes that gun away from Adams?"

Leaning forward, keeping his gun steady as a rock, Lee snatched the pistol from Clint's holster and stepped back. Once he was a safe distance away, Lee held Clint's customized gun in front of him and looked it over while letting out a slow whistle. "This is a nice piece of work," he said. "I don't know whether I should keep it after you're dead or sell it off. I'm sure someone would pay a good price for The Gunsmith's pistol."

Clint looked over to Mandy. The younger Respit was busy tying her to a chair, and seemed to be doing his best not to hurt her. Consequently, his knots were not very good. She kept her head held high and her eyes focused straight ahead. Tears glistened at the corners of her eyes, but she didn't let them fall down her cheeks.

"Why don't you just tell me what you want so we can get on with this?" Clint asked.

Sheriff Kenrick stepped all the way into the room, pulling the rope along with him. Tied to the end, with his hands bound and a gag in his mouth, was Professor Henry Whiteoak. Judging by the way he stumbled over his feet and nearly ran into the door frame, Whiteoak was either drunk or so dead tired that he could barely stand. When Clint got a better look at the professor's face, he could tell that Whiteoak had been beaten no more than a few hours ago.

Both of the man's eyes were covered with purple bruises, swelling up until his eyelids were half shut. A thick collection of blood was drying at the corner of his mouth, and a knot was swelling up just below Whiteoak's hatband.

Clint held Whiteoak's gaze, and could almost hear the other man's thoughts. He had the look of a tired, whipped dog that had been choking on its own blood while being tied to a post in the rain. And as much as Clint hated to admit it . . . he actually felt sorry for the man.

When Lee's fist slammed into the side of Clint's face, he knew that Whiteoak wasn't just a human being in need, but a glimpse into his own painful future.

EIGHTEEN

Smitty Evanston was not a brave man. He was, however, tired of hiding. He hadn't been laying low for more than a few days, but it seemed as though it had been years since his life had been able to ride along at its own pace. He hadn't been able to eat at his normal haunts or drink at his favorite saloon. Even sleeping in his bed came with some degree of fear brought on by the threats of the Respit brothers.

Finally, as the sun rose high enough to peek over the barn stall that Smitty had been calling home, the stocky ex-miner stood up, dusted the hay from his shoulders and legs, and made a decision. He decided not to be afraid anymore. And even though all of Professor Whiteoak's miracle tonic was long gone, Smitty swore he could still feel the courage in that bottle trickling through his veins.

His gun was still back at home, which was a little over a mile walk from where he was hiding out. If he thought this surge of nerve would last more than a few minutes, Smitty might have run up to the house to get the pistol he'd used to shoot Owen Respit. But he knew himself too well. He was certain that by the time he made it home, it would take a miracle to get him out again.

No, what he needed to do was get some help. Or at least get someone to lend him a gun. Seeing as how his steady hand had left him after the potion had worn off, Smitty decided to go with the first option. He couldn't think of anyone better for help than Sheriff Kenrick. That young man seemed like the sort that would be willing to listen to an old man's ramblings. Smitty knew he might be looking at some jail time for shooting Owen, but that was all part of a good man paying his dues.

Besides, he knew there were plenty of people who'd witnessed the fight. It was a fair one and Owen had lost. Simple as that.

Taking a deep breath, Smitty forced himself to stop thinking of ways to justify his actions and to just go on and do them. The first step, he knew, was walking out of the stall. He reached out and removed the latch keeping the gate closed. He was still covered with a fine layer of dust, and blades of straw jabbed through his clothes like little stingers, making him itch all over his body. The barn was being used as a livery now, which meant that he smelled a lot like the animals he'd slept with over the past few nights. But Smitty knew there wasn't anything he could do about that . . . not before he took care of his business and got his life back on track.

As he walked proudly out of that empty horse's stall, Smitty thought back to earlier in the day when he'd seen that man come in to visit the Darley Arabian next door. There was something about that one that had almost made him sit up and introduce himself. He'd watched the other man sneak out the back, poke around the professor's wagon, and then leave with something tucked under his arm.

He didn't know who the man was or what he'd taken from that wagon, but Smitty didn't much care. All he did care about was finding that man and offering a simple trade. He wouldn't tell about what he'd seen if that man would protect him from the Respits.

Smitty had seen the gun on that man's hip, and knew it was some kind of modified Colt. He also knew that a man didn't carry a gun like that unless he knew how to use it. So if Sheriff Kenrick wouldn't help, Smitty knew he had another option. And that, more than anything else, was what gave him the courage to get up and leave his hiding place. He may have sunk to sleeping in horse manure and spying from shadows. He may have even started to turn into an extortionist to save his own hide, but Smitty Evanston was not about to let a man like Lee Respit get the better of him.

Maybe there was some of that potion left in his system after all, he thought. Or maybe there was something in that vile concoction that had just eaten away enough of his brain to make him crazy.

Whatever it was, Smitty was just glad to get out of that damn stall.

Five men rode out of Grand Junction, Colorado, heading west toward the state line. They'd taken a train all the way from Cheyenne, opting to ride the rest of the way into Chester on their own. It was always easier that way on a job. They didn't like having to wait for trains or stages to get them out of town when they could ride out as soon as their contract was fulfilled.

None of them spoke to each other. They'd been working together so long that there was hardly anything left to say. They all knew what each other was thinking, which was part of the reason they could charge so much for their services.

They were more than a team. They were a well-oiled machine.

They headed off on their way to Chester, Utah, already knowing what they would do once they got there, how long it would take, and how they would get out of town. All that remained was the tedious detail of actually following through on their actions. They were going to Chester to prove a point and reclaim property that had been stolen right out from under them.

It wasn't a good idea to steal from men like these.

Henry Whiteoak needed to learn that.

Emily Tate had spent the last three days on a stagecoach coming up from Tombstone. It seemed as though the driver had stopped in every backwater village that broke the road, just to make the trip seem longer than it had to be. All the while, she'd had to endure countless hours of the old man with the thick spectacles leering at her from across the cramped and jostling carriage. That old man with the banker's suit and greasy hair never once paid attention to his poor wife, who prattled on endlessly about recipes and the weather.

Emily had sat there and listened to the older woman's boring anecdotes, pretending to be interested in topics that should have interested any fine, upstanding girl. She'd sat there and politely turned her head when the banker leaned forward for the twentieth time to adjust shoelaces that were already tied just to get a closer look at her ample breasts. She'd even pretended not to notice when that banker had patted her behind as they'd stopped to water the horses at some broken-down village on the state line.

She'd been real polite and tolerant . . . for the first day of the trip.

The second day, she'd allowed her dress to slip high up around her legs, and then adjusted her posture just enough to make that banker's eyes bug out of his head. Then, she'd caught the older woman's attention just as her husband was leering from his position bent over his shoes.

Caught red-handed, the banker and anyone else in earshot of his wife got a hearty portion of her ranting and crying at her husband. The older woman yelled at him for hours, giving him a verbal beating for everything ranging from past affairs to his inadequacies in the bedroom, making the older man squirm like an uncomfortable sinner in church.

It was rather entertaining, but not enough to distract Emily from the reason she was on that stage to begin with.

After a while, she'd busied herself by braiding long strands of her reddish-blond hair, humming to herself until the squabbling couple faded away into obscurity. Emily stared out the little window of the bouncing stage, thinking about the work that waited for her in Chester and the life of luxury she could lead once that work was done.

Every time she crossed her legs, she could feel the stiffness of the two-shot derringer tied to the inside of her thigh. The gun had been warmed by her skin until the steel felt like another part of her body. The pearl handle felt smooth against her flesh, rubbing high up her leg like a lover's finger. She thought about the times when that gun had gone off in her hands, and a warm flush tinted her cheeks.

Sometimes, as the carriage rumbled through the end of the day and the sun was dipping low on the horizon, Emily would shift her legs until the gun's pearl handle was just barely touching the sensitive spot between her legs. Even after a day's worth of browbeating, that banker would still stare at her, and when she felt the little pistol brushing against her moistening lips, she would smile at him and move her leg back and forth over her knee, savoring the feel of the weapon and the warm dampness it created beneath her skirt.

Only a few miles remained now before they entered the town of Chester. Emily looked out the window at the afternoon sun and thought about what awaited her. She crossed her legs, just as she'd done the night before, and gently swung her foot between the coach's seats. The gun worked its way up her leg with every practiced swing until its handle nearly pushed inside her. Emily closed her eyes and kept up her motion until little waves of pleasure caused her to shudder. She thought about that gun kicking in her hand, and had to bite her lip to keep herself from crying out.

NINETEEN

Henry Whiteoak sat slumped over in a chair, sitting in the same position as when he'd been dumped there fifteen minutes ago. Although it had only been a quarter of an hour, Clint felt every second as it dragged by, punctuated by the slamming of Lee's fist into his face or body.

Only the first few blows really hurt much. After that, they stung just enough to keep Clint's eyes open and a fire burning deep in his gut. He used that fire to take his mind off the splitting of his lip and the bruising of his ribs. All the while, he glared across the room at Sheriff Kenrick, who was covering him with a Winchester rifle, waiting for Clint to make a move in the wrong direction.

Clint knew better than to oblige the crooked lawman. That would come later. His hands had been tied, but the job was done in a hurry, and Clint had already managed to wrangle his wrists all but free from their bonds.

"Why are you doing this?" Mandy asked through the layer of tears that had all but covered her face.

Nickolas Respit leaned forward and put a hand on her shoulder. "Jus' be quiet now," he said softly. "We ain't here to hurt you none."

Lee reared back his fist, and was about to send it crashing into Clint's nose when Kenrick's voice boomed through the entire office.

"Enough!" Kenrick ordered. The sheriff stepped in front of Lee and held his rifle in the crook of his arm. He started to get a smile on his face, but quickly got rid of it when he caught a glimpse of the deadly look that Clint was wearing. "Trust me, Adams, if I'd have known you were going to be in town, none of this would have been happening yet. I got nothing against you, but you wound up in a place you shouldn't have been."

"Is that supposed to make me feel better?" Clint asked.

Lee was walking over to Mandy, rubbing his bloody knuckles. "I know something that would make me feel better," he said while glaring at the quiet woman. "And I don't mind at all bein' second in line."

"Stay away from her, Lee," Kenrick said without taking his eyes away from Clint. He shifted on his feet and took up the gun in both hands. Aiming at Clint's head, the lawman stood his ground and let the silence grow thick in the air.

The voice that broke it was hoarse and ragged. It came from a part of the room that had been all but forgotten during the last few minutes. "Why don't we cut through all this horseshit and get to the damn point?"

Everyone turned toward the corner of the room where Henry Whiteoak was propped up in his chair next to the door leading to the jail cells. The professor's hands were tied behind his back and his body was slumped forward. His head was shaking from the effort of holding it up, yet his eyes radiated a strength bred from pure anger.

"This could have all gone so much easier," Whiteoak said, "if one of you would have just skipped the bravado and gone straight to the reason why you're doing all of this. Hell, Kenrick, you might have been able to get out of it without tipping your hand."

The sheriff turned toward Whiteoak and started to say something, but was cut short when Clint sprang from his chair, snapped his wrists from the ropes, and grabbed for the rifle in Kenrick's hands. Suddenly, the room was a flurry of movement as Lee pivoted on his heels and began tugging the pistol from his holster. Mandy jumped into action the moment Lee looked away, and threw herself at the big man, trying to snatch the gun from him. Watching all of this unfold in front of him, Nickolas Respit instinctively started to step away from it, just like he did at home whenever violence began to show itself.

Like a seasoned pro in the art of stirring up trouble, Whiteoak chose the perfect moment to duck out of harm's way and throw himself to the ground. His body hit the floor with a painful thud. With his hands still tied behind his back, his face wound up slamming against the wood before anything else, but it didn't prevent him from rolling to the side until his back was up against a wall.

Clint couldn't feel anything but the need to take advantage of the opening Whiteoak had created. His ribs throbbed inside his torso and his head pounded in agony, but none of that registered as he moved like a flicker, throwing himself at Sheriff Kenrick. Before he knew it, the rifle was in his hands and his entire upper body was twisting to the side until the weapon was ripped out of Kenrick's fists. Once Clint had ahold of the rifle and twisted it away, his momentum staggered him back in the opposite direction just as a shot exploded in the air.

Kenrick was stumbling backward also, and could feel the hot lead whip past his head like an angry hornet.

At the other end of the room, Mandy held on to Lee's gun and pointed it in the sheriff's general direction. Smoke curled up from the barrel, and a look of panic was etched across her suddenly pale face. As soon as she saw that she'd nearly blown the head off a man, her arms went limp and the gun dropped to the floor.

"Mandy, get down," Clint yelled over the ringing in his ears.

She did as she was told, and covered her head with her hands. She then crawled across the floor to seek shelter beneath Kenrick's desk.

Clint saw that the sheriff had gotten over the initial shock and was about to start fighting back. Turning sharply, Clint sent the stock of the Winchester slamming hard into Kenrick's gut. The sheriff let out all his air with a pained grunt, doubling over like a doll that had been folded in half.

Without missing a beat, Clint brought the rifle up to his shoulder, levered in a round, and sighted down the barrel toward the other end of the room. He saw Nickolas Respit pressing himself back against the locked door. The younger man had gotten his gun out, but held the weapon like an old man gripping his cane, letting it hang from his fist like an accessory.

Clint shifted to the next man in sight. Lee Respit was crouching down to make a grab for his pistol, which was on the floor, and Clint didn't even bother shouting out a warning before squeezing the rifle's trigger. The gun bucked against his shoulder once, spitting out a puff of smoke and a chunk of lead that flew from the barrel and through the air to take a bite out of Lee's right shoulder.

"Goddamn!" Lee screamed as he was thrown off the balls of his feet to bounce against Kenrick's desk.

Clint worked the Winchester's lever while pivoting to check on what was going on behind him. Whiteoak was keeping himself well out of harm's way, while Sheriff Kenrick was making a grab for his holster.

"Don't," Clint warned as he swung the rifle around to aim at the sheriff.

"You're no outlaw," Kenrick said evenly. "I know you don't make a habit of shooting lawmen."

"You gave up your right to wear that badge the minute you decided to use it for whatever mess you're wrapped up in right now." Clint positioned himself so that he could see everyone in the room except for Mandy, who was still hiding beneath the desk. "Why don't you do me a favor and toss that pistol this way, Sheriff."

Kenrick slowly took out his other gun and pitched it toward Clint's feet.

"Now disarm those two," Clint said while motioning toward the Respits, "and lock them in jail where they belong."

Nickolas seemed relieved to be inside the cage, more so when he saw his brother wasn't going to be locked inside with him. Rather, Lee got his own cell, and began cursing loudly the minute Clint led the sheriff back out to the office.

"It's not too late, you know," Kenrick said after he was sitting down in the chair Whiteoak had abandoned.

Clint went through the desk drawers until he found his own gun, and slid it back into its holster. He kept the rifle in hand, but let it hang at his side rather than pointed at the sheriff's face. "Too late for what?"

Kenrick paused for a second to take a slow, pained breath. He gripped the spot where Clint had hit him with the rifle stock, and winced. "I'm sorry about Lee. I figured if I let him rough you up a bit, it would be enough to cool him down. He wanted to kill you, but I wasn't about to let him."

Clint's voice dripped with sarcasm. "How generous of you. Why not just give me an explanation? Maybe then you can convince me to give you another chance." Pausing for a second, Clint brought the rifle back up to bear on Sheriff Kenrick and snapped the safety off with a flick of his thumb. "But after the day I've had, I'd say you've got a pretty tough job ahead of you."

At that moment, the door to the office busted in and two young men who couldn't have been more than twenty years old came charging through with guns drawn. Clint's reflex was to turn and cover them with the rifle, but he stopped short when he saw the deputy's badges on their shirts.

The deputy first through the door looked excited and ready for a fight. His barrel chest huffed and his blue eyes were wide and searching. "We heard shooting, Sheriff," he said. "Are you all right?"

"You're just in time," Kenrick said as he got up and walked casually toward Clint. "There was a bit of a problem with one of our prisoners and the Respit brothers. Mr. Adams here was just helping me deal with the situation." He stood over Clint and held his hands out. "My rifle, please."

Clint knew he had two choices at that particular point in time. He could take over the sheriff's job by force, and probably have to fight both of the eager deputies, or he could choose the solution that would keep everyone in the room alive and healthy. A bitter taste formed in the back of Clint's mouth as he stood up and looked directly into the sheriff's eyes.

He swore he could feel bile rising in the back of his throat when he ejected the cartridges from the rifle and handed it over. "This isn't over," he said.

Kenrick took the rifle and looked over his shoulder toward the jail cells. "Oh, I know that. But don't worry, we handle our own business. Now that everyone's cards are on the table, we'll wrap this up properly."

Lowering his voice so that he could only be heard by the sheriff, Clint said, "If you even try to get me in one of those cells—"

"I meant what I said, Adams. We'll finish this soon. I just blew my own chances to arrest you without suspicion, but don't make the mistake of thinking that you're safe."

Clint stared daggers through the crooked lawman's skull, and didn't let up until Kenrick took a few steps back by way of submission. "Come on, Mandy," Clint said. "It's time for us to go."

He helped the petrified woman climb out from her hiding space, and walked right past the confused deputies.

"Thanks again for your help, Adams," Kenrick said before they made it through the door.

Fighting back the urge to turn around and take care of the sheriff for good, Clint stopped after Mandy had walked outside. "Come on, Whiteoak. Let's get you cleaned up."

Rather than explain to his deputies what the professor was doing out of his cell, Kenrick allowed the con man to go. "I'll be checking on you," he said to Whiteoak. "Real soon."

TWENTY

Clint did his best to ignore Whiteoak's rambling as he led the professor and Mandy away from the sheriff's office toward one of the hotels he'd spotted as he'd wandered around town. It was on the way to the livery and no more than a block or two away from Mil's. The hotel was nearly full, but he managed to get a room with a window facing the street, which was all Clint really wanted.

"I can't say this enough," Whiteoak said for the hundredth time. "From the bottom of my heart, thank you so much for removing me from that godforsaken cage. I swear, that sheriff meant to do me harm the likes of which—"

"Henry," Clint interrupted, "shut up."

It was obviously a great effort, but the professor managed to choke back whatever he was about to say, and took a seat on the edge of the room's creaky bed. Mandy had been holding up rather well, but as soon as she got behind closed doors, the tears came back to her eyes and she rushed over to Clint. Her arms wrapped around his neck and she buried her face in his shirt.

"I was so scared," she sobbed. "I thought we were all gonna die. And I thought Sheriff Kenrick was a good man."

Clint let her sob for a little while before easing her over to the bed and setting her down. "It's going to be all right," he said. "Kenrick may be a skunk, but I've seen his kind so many times before. It still makes me sick when lawmen like that poke their heads out of the grass."

Whiteoak had removed a handkerchief from his shirt pocket, and was dabbing at the cut on the corner of his mouth. He raised his hand and shook it in the air, saying, "I second that notion. So I take it that you've decided to put some faith in my word, Adams?"

Clint took a folded rag from a small beside table and dipped it into the cool water that was in a small washbasin on the floor. He wrung it out and handed it over to Mandy. "I'm not going to go that far, Whiteoak, but I will say that there seems to be a kernel of truth in what you said."

"Of course, I would never—"

"But make no mistake," Clint said as he stood in front of Whiteoak and glared down at him. "I know as well as anyone that the best lies are the ones that have that kernel of truth in the center. And if I find out that you're trying to string me along, I'll be very, very upset." His hand drifted toward his gun and hung there like a specter. "Am I being perfectly clear?"

Whiteoak swallowed painfully, choking on the threat as well as a fair amount of his own blood. "Certainly."

"Good. Now, since I've committed myself to this mess, why don't we start by bringing everyone up to date on what's truly going on here."

Sighing, Whiteoak said, "I already told you every-thing. . . ."

"Then you'll tell me again."

There was a chair next to the room's single window, and Clint pulled this up so he could take a seat facing the pro-fessor. He sat there and listened as Whiteoak retold his story, which pretty much matched the one he'd told Clint from his jail cell. All the while, Clint was listening to every word, waiting for the other man to trip himself up with contradic-tions or anything that didn't match when compared to what had already been said.

Rather than getting a clear sign that Whiteoak was lying, Clint became more and more convinced that the man was telling the truth. Mandy seemed to be getting ahold of herself while also listening to the professor talk. She leaned forward on the bed and watched Whiteoak as he gestured with his hands, adding colorful details as he became more and more comfortable in his surroundings.

Finally, the story came full circle and Whiteoak began getting into what had happened after he'd talked to Clint the first time.

"After you left, I thought for sure that my luck was about to change," Whiteoak said with a smile on his face. "The last time we met, we seemed to somehow turn things around just when I was starting to think that I was at the end of my rope."

"Wait a second," Mandy interrupted. "You two know each other?"

"Unfortunately, yes," Clint said. "I got involved in a scuffle thanks to a particularly dangerous con the good professor here was running."

"What happened?"

Clint saw Whiteoak take a deep breath in preparation for another one of his long-winded stories. Rather than waste another hour on such a tale, he cut Whiteoak off at the pass. "Seems ol' Henry here swindled a land baron out of a large enough sum of money that three killers were sent after him. Those men rode over and through anyone who happened to stand between them and their target, killing folks rather than asking them to step aside. And thanks again to the professor, he nearly got us both killed just so he could pull off the job, even though he could have walked away from it more than once without hurting more than his pride.

"Oh, and I believe there was also a matter of him almost getting lynched for cheating at cards and poisoning people with his miracle tonics so that he could rob them even easier while they were passed out." Clint hadn't broken eye contact with Whiteoak this entire time. He saw the man had been dying to jump in to defend himself, but had become less anxious as Clint rattled off his story. "Does that sound about right to you, Professor?"

Now that he'd been given his chance to speak, Whiteoak lifted his chin and assumed a posture as though he was about to address a classroom. But by the time he'd turned around to face Mandy, he'd lost his steam and allowed a guilty look to creep into his eyes. "Yeah," he said without any of the bluster that normally infused his voice. "I guess that about covers it."

Clint took no small amount of satisfaction from cracking Whiteoak's facade. Just seeing the con man cornered into even the smallest admission of his wrongdoing was a pleasure that he remembered fondly from their last encounter years ago. "And now I'm supposed to help you again," Clint said, "Why should I?"

This time, when Whiteoak turned back to look at Clint, his expression was filled with genuine concern. It was a difference that was almost startling compared to the normal show the professor put on. "Why should you help me? Because I'll die if you don't, Adams. It's as simple as that."

Clint started to say something, but it was Whiteoak who interrupted him this time.

"I know what I've done in the past," the professor said. "And I'm not going to insult your intelligence by sitting here and giving you an apology. I ply my trade to make a living . . . that's all there is to it. Sometimes I steal and other times I cheat, but rest assured I always pay for my way of life one way or another.

"But this time I've stumbled on something that just might let me park that wagon of mine for good. Those deeds I told you about are genuine and I won them fair and square."

"Well . . ." Clint started.

Whiteoak raised his hands. "All right. Let's just say I won them. The point is, I got those deeds the way a lot of others get theirs and they belong to me. I didn't make them up and I'm not trying to con someone else into buying them. And as much as you hate to admit it, Adams, you know that I'm telling the truth."

Whiteoak was right about one thing. Clint most definitely hated to admit that the professor was actually on the level this time.

"All right, Whiteoak," Clint said. "I may be making a big mistake, but I'm going to go along with you on this one. But this is just because we seem to have a common enemy here. You better count yourself lucky that I can't abide crooked lawmen any more than I can abide you. So what I propose is not so much of a partnership but an agreement.

"We work together to get to the bottom of what's going on with those deeds and the people involved with them. Your part is to tell me what I need to know and earn the ticket out of jail I gave to you."

"Of course."

"You'll pay your fine out of your own pocket and walk free like any other man who settled up in the eyes of the law."

"No problem, but first I need to get to my—"

"I've been to your wagon and have got your money."

Whiteoak's eyes lit up like candles in a dark room.

"Before you get too excited," Clint said, "I'm keeping that money myself, minus the price of the fine, which I'll hand over personally. Think of that as my own insurance policy to keep you from running too far."

Standing up, Whiteoak smiled widely through the bloody smears on his face and the dark bruises around his eyes. He held out a hand to Clint, who looked up at him from his chair as though he wasn't sure whether to shake the hand or bat it away.

"I appreciate this, Clint. I honestly do."

Clint nodded, shook Whiteoak's hand, and wondered if he was helping a man in need or playing poker with a deck he already knew was loaded.

TWENTY-ONE

For the time being, Clint didn't want Mandy or Whiteoak to show their faces on the street. With the local sheriff working with the likes of the Respits, Clint wasn't all too comfortable walking on the streets himself. He wasn't worried about his own safety so much as being forced into a shootout with one of Kenrick's deputies. So far, those deputies seemed to be following orders as best as they could. The fact that Kenrick had lied to them was enough to convince Clint that the other lawmen in Chester were simply doing their duty.

He'd done his best when getting the hotel room to make sure he'd been seen signing the register. Clint had made no effort to hide the fact that he was renting a room there, but he did a damn good job of sneaking Mandy and Whiteoak out of the place and into an alley where all three made their way to a secluded spot behind the hotel.

"This should be enough to throw anyone looking for us off the mark," Clint said. "At least for a little while." He turned to Mandy and took her by the hands. "You don't have any part in this," he said to her. "I want you to keep out of sight until this all gets settled. I'd rather you didn't go home, because if Kenrick wants to find you, that'll be the first place he looks. Hopefully, this hotel will be the second. Now, do you have a place to stay in the meantime?"

She thought about that for a few moments, and then her

face brightened. "Sam's got a place just outside of town. He'll put me up for a while."

"Are you sure about that?"

Mandy nodded. "I got him his job cooking at Mil's. He owes me."

"Then we'll get you over there first thing. If we want to contact each other, we'll do it through Sam at the restaurant."

"I can get there through a back way. It's just right through this next alley." Mandy turned to leave, then stopped and went back to Clint, hugging him with a surprising amount of strength. "Be careful," she said. "I've got a bad feeling that something's gonna go wrong with all of this."

Clint held on to her, and ran his fingers through her hair. He then lifted her chin until he could kiss her softly on the lips. "You just watch yourself and I'll take care of the rest. Don't worry about me. You'll hear from me by tonight."

She pressed her lips against his, tasting him with soft, tantalizing strokes of her tongue inside Clint's mouth. "We'll both feel a lot better tonight," she whispered. "Even better than last night."

After one more quick kiss, Mandy turned and took off down the alley, which opened up on the next street over from the hotel. Clint watched as she hurried out into the empty street past the mouth of the alley, then ducked in between another set of buildings.

"So what now?" Whiteoak asked.

"Now I want to get a closer look at what this whole damn mess is about."

Before Whiteoak could say anything, Clint was walking behind the building next to the hotel, knowing full well that the professor would stay close by. It took him a minute to get his bearings, but when he did, Clint knew that he was only about two streets over from where the body of Owen Respit had been lying. They were halfway there when Whiteoak broke the silence between them.

"You're going to check out one of my properties?"

Clint nodded, easing out of the alley and onto a boardwalk within sight of the corpse. "That's right." Once the wind shifted, it blew a pungent odor right into Clint's face that made his toes curl inside his boots and his stomach lurch in protest. "I still don't see what the purpose of that is," Clint said, indicating the body.

They were standing on a corner separating the living and dead parts of town. Clint leaned against a post supporting an awning in front of a small dry goods store, while Whiteoak tried to look inconspicuous behind him.

"Lee's an opportunist," Whiteoak said. "But nobody ever accused him of being very subtle. He wants people to stay away from that property and that's what they're doing."

"And I suppose he knew that Owen was going to get shot right in that spot?"

Whiteoak laughed under his breath and removed his handkerchief to cover his nose. "I know that Owen wasn't the family favorite, but I doubt he was supposed to get himself killed. I think Lee just lucked out in that his brother happened to get caught on his way out from inspecting that property."

Clint turned to look at Whiteoak. "Is that what he was doing there when he got shot?"

"Owen was usually there when Lee and I talked business, but he did some of the inspecting as well. They weren't close, but Lee would get upset whenever someone made trouble for anyone in his family."

"Yeah. So upset that he decided to use his brother's body to keep people away."

Another stifled laugh came from Whiteoak. "You always did have a way of cutting through the bullshit, Adams. I got to admit that I admire that about you." The professor took a few steps forward, which put him right beside Clint. "You've dealt with dangerous men enough to know that they don't always think in straight lines. They may not all be crazy, but they just don't work like anyone else. They survive by using whatever they get. That's how they can justify doing the things they do."

"I'm sure you know all about that."

"That's right," Whiteoak said without so much as a moment's hesitation. "I know a hell of a lot about that, which is why you want me to help you on this one rather than locking me up someplace to keep me out of the way. Am I right?"

"I haven't quite made my mind up about you, Professor," Clint said without taking his eyes off the people that walked back and forth across the street. "That's why I'm keeping you close by where I can watch you like a hawk. You slip up once and you'll be back in chains faster than you can blink."

"I know, I know. You told me that already."

"Yeah, well, I also told you to keep your nose clean the last time we parted ways, and look how well you listened to that advice."

For the moment, there seemed to be a lull in the amount of people passing by on the street. Clint walked across until he was close enough to see the patch of dry, blackened blood on Owen's shirt. He could hear the sound of Whiteoak's footsteps following behind him even over the constant buzz of insects swarming around the rancid body. Holding his breath against the stench, Clint took a closer look at the body before hurrying to the storefront and trying the door.

It was locked.

"Here . . ." Whiteoak said while doing his best to hold back his gag reflex. "Allow me." The professor then produced a key from his pocket, and slipped it into the lock beneath the door's handle.

The door swung open on noisy hinges and both men stepped inside. Once the place was closed up and locked again, Clint tried taking another breath. The air inside was better, but still carried the taint of fermenting meat. "And how'd you keep the sheriff from finding that?" he asked while pointing to the key in Whiteoak's hand.

"I've got enough pockets in these clothes to carry around a small store without anyone knowing any better."

The inside of the place looked as though it had been struck by a tornado. Tables had been overturned and shoved against the walls. Shelves and racks of all sizes littered the floor after having been reduced to kindling. Rats scurried noisily from one side of the room to another, finding ample places to hide within piles of dusty garbage.

"I've got to hand it to you, Whiteoak. You sure know how to pick your investments. This is a prime piece of real estate you've got here." Clint kicked over what had at one time been a bookshelf, and revealed the remains of a cat that had been picked clean by the local vermin. "I can sure see what all the fuss is about, although I don't think Lee had to do much to keep people away from this place."

"It's not all this that everyone's after, Adams. It's what—"

"It's me that they're after," said a voice from the back of the room that brought Clint's hand reflexively to the gun in his holster.

"Come out where we can see you," Clint said, his body tensed and ready for action.

In the far corner of the room, there was a counter that had probably been where the owners of the store had kept the cash register. A figure straightened up from behind the counter and started walking around the mildewed wood. "I'm the one that started all this," said a stocky older man with a face full of gray whiskers. "And I aim to help finish it."

TWENTY-TWO

The stage rumbled into Chester amid a flurry of galloping hooves and clouds of dust. It pulled to a stop in front of the town's largest hotel, which was called the River's Lodge, situated across from the only place in town that ran more than two poker tables at once. The driver reined his team to a halt and climbed down from the top of the stage. His partner made his way onto the roof of the carriage, and began pulling down baggage and tossing it to the ground.

The door to the stage swung open, allowing an older man in a distinguished suit to make his way outside. After a quick look around, he reached back inside the coach and helped his wife to make her way down the metal folding steps.

"Looks like a nice enough place," said the old man. "At least for one night until we can hop onto the stage to California." After his wife was out and on her feet, he reached back inside the coach to aid another woman through the small door.

Unlike the first woman, this one seemed to have the man's full attention as she extended a leg from the coach and put her weight onto the top step below the door. Black leather boots covered her feet, extending all the way to her knees. Although they could only be seen for an instant as she drew up her skirts to keep from falling, those legs seemed more than enough to please the old banker.

"Thank you," Emily said sweetly as she stepped down from the coach and took her hand out of the banker's grasp. She got the old man to keep his eyes on her a few seconds too many, and smiled when the man's wife clubbed him on the back of his head with her handbag.

"I swear to the Lord above, if I see you doing that again . . ." the older woman fumed while grabbing hold of her husband's collar. She dragged him away and into the hotel before the banker could even get ahold of his bags.

Emily Tate waited patiently until her valise was dropped to the ground, and bent daintily at the knees to pick it up. The derringer was nestled firmly between her thighs, and the sides of the gun pressed like a cool hand sliding beneath her skirts. Her body had warmed the pearl handle so that the weapon felt like it was a part of herself. When she stood back up, she kept her legs together, moving the gun a little further down her thigh.

"You need any help with that, ma'am?" the driver asked as he walked around his team.

Emily knew the big driver had been watching her whenever she sauntered into his line of sight. Since she had no use for him, she only showed him half a smile and didn't meet his eyes. "No, but thank you kindly. I'll just be staying right here."

The driver started to say something else, but she ignored what was probably a ham-handed proposition and walked inside the River's Lodge.

The hotel wasn't much compared to what any of the bigger cities had to offer, but the lobby was clean enough and there didn't seem to be a lot of traffic going through the place. Emily walked up to the register, paid for her room, and signed her name before heading for the stairs.

Her room was on the third floor and looked out onto the roof of the gaming parlor across the street. After having been trapped inside the hot confines of the stagecoach with the smell of the old banker forcing itself into her lungs, she was glad to lock herself inside her room and peel off the layers of clothing until she was down to a plain white shift that was soaked with her own sweat and clinging to her body.

There was a small oval mirror set on top of a four-drawer

dresser. Emily walked to the window and pulled the blind down all the way. As her hands drifted over her body, she turned toward the washbasin sitting on a small round table in the corner. She cupped her hands, filled them with water, and splashed it over her body. The shift clung to her large, rounded breasts, and when she looked down at herself, Emily could see her nipples hardening from the chill of the water. The material became a second skin, and when she walked across the room, the thick patch of blond hair between her legs could be seen through her slip.

She giggled like a naughty little girl as she opened the window to let in some air and left the blinds halfway open. Imagining that someone was watching her, Emily slowly moved the thin straps off her shoulder and peeled the top of her slip down to her waist. Once she was in front of the mirror, she ran her hands over her body.

Emily stood there for a few moments, savoring the feel of her own touch and thinking about all that awaited her. She knew her entire life was going to change. When she left Chester, she wouldn't be the same person as when she'd arrived.

She gently ran the tips of her fingernails over her breasts, tracing a line beneath the rounded curve of her flesh and down over her ribs. When she got to her stomach, she moved her hands so that the tips of her fingers were pushing down toward her pelvis until they slid just beneath her slip. A soft moan came from her lips as she pressed harder and moved her hands down lower. The thin cotton slip moved down her body as well, pushed along by her probing hands. Finally, she could feel the thick patch of soft hair between her fingers, and she lingered there, swaying back and forth.

Emily opened her eyes languidly, taking in the sight of herself in the oval mirror. Her body was slick with perspiration and strands of her hair stuck to her moist forehead. Moving her hands back up her body, she walked toward the window, leaving the slip in place hanging halfway down her hips. As she walked, she moved her legs so that she could feel the gun shifting against her skin, the metal growing just a little colder as she walked past the incoming breeze.

With both hands, she slid the cotton slip down over her

hips and let it drop to the floor. Naked except for the black lace garter that held the derringer to her thigh, Emily stepped out of the fallen garment and walked over to the edge of her bed. Once there, she lowered herself onto the mattress, leaned forward so that the ends of her hair tickled the tops of her thighs, and spread her legs slowly enough to feel the muscles moving beneath her skin.

She loved to look at herself, imagining how many men had caught sight of her and wished they could see what she saw at this moment. A smile crept across her face as she reached down to pluck the derringer from its little holster. She didn't let the gun break contact with her skin as she slid it up and along her thigh. The metal felt cool against her flesh, and downright cold once it touched the sensitive skin beneath the downy thatch of blond hair between her legs. Shudders began traveling up her back and her legs stiffened on the edge of the bed. She leaned back, supporting herself with one arm as her eyes clenched shut and her mouth opened to let out a slow groan.

She moved the gun up and down faster now, savoring the way it slid easier between her legs, slipping luxuriously in her moisture. The very notion of what that gun could do, combined with the motion of it between her legs, brought Emily to the brink of ecstasy. She was moaning louder now, and before her hands moved faster than she could control, she let the gun drop to the floor and allowed her body to fall back onto the bed.

One hand kept working between her thighs until the pleasure consumed her entire being and every part of her trembled with sheer delight. She kept her hands pressed tightly against her body until the orgasm subsided, waiting for just the right moment to move her hands in just the right spots to bring about another.

Exhausted, she lay on top of the covers, enjoying the feel of a breeze running over her naked body. She dozed off for a few minutes, and when she awoke, she slipped into a clean dress and tied her hair back with a red ribbon. The derringer fit snugly in a garter that was made out of matching red lace and hung above her knee as though she'd been born to carry it there.

There was still much to be done and precious little time in which to do it. Everything seemed so exciting now. Her heart pounded excitedly in her chest and her brain raced, all of it fueled by just a hint of fear.

To get her hands on all that money, she would have to put herself amid a lot of dangerous men. She might even not make it out of Chester alive.

Just thinking about it sent a delicious chill down through her body.

TWENTY-THREE

Smitty Evanston stepped from the shadows with his head bowed and his hands folded in front of his body. Despite the gray hair, full beard, and stocky frame, he looked like a guilty child who was merely waiting for the leather strap to fall. He walked around the counter and stood in front of Clint and Whiteoak as though they were a firing line.

"I never thought anything like this would happen," Smitty said. "I'm sorry."

"Sorry for what?" Clint asked.

The older man looked around for something to sit on, found a stack of dirty crates, and lowered himself down onto the precariously balanced boxes. "Owen and I had our scuffles. We went around whenever we saw each other, but everyone always told me to just let it pass. Then he started hittin' me . . . roughing me up if I so much as set foot in the wrong place.

"M'wife told me that I wasn't much of a man for letting someone do that to me. But she's a woman and don't understand how things go in the world. Owen knew well enough, though. He knew he could do whatever he wanted to me 'cause his brothers would always be there to back his play. 'Sides, I never was much of a fightin' man."

Clint knew the story even before the words came from Smitty's mouth. As long as there were more than a few hu-

98

mans in one place, there would always be those trying to work their way to the top of the heap. Whether it was through politics, money, or simply beating down those weaker than them, those men would try any way they could to make themselves seem more than what they were.

The only difference was in which men earned their status and which ones merely pretended to have it.

"I heard about what happened," Clint said. "It sounded like a clean fight to me, Smitty. At least, as clean as something like this could ever be."

"There ain't nothin' clean about it, mister." Shaking his head, Smitty hunched his shoulders and stared down at the gritty floor. "Every time I see that body outside, I know I'm next. I can smell death in this town an' it's all my fault. I've been keepin' low and tryin' to stay outta sight, but I can still hear folks when they walk by.

"They see that body there and they want to hand me over just so's they can clear it out. Lee won't let nobody near it, and he's already beat the hell outta three men jus' for lookin' at it the wrong way." Smitty took a deep breath and looked up at Clint. "Maybe I should just take my medicine."

Shaking his head, Clint walked over to the older man and set a hand on his shoulder. "That's exactly what Lee wants. He figures he'll rub your face in this until you can't take it anymore and make a mistake. I've been wondering what could possess a man to do that, but it all just boils down to one thing. Lee's too damn lazy to look for you, so he's making you come to him."

Smitty didn't seem to hear much of what anyone else was saying. Instead, his eyes tracked from one side of the room to another and he began wringing his hands nervously. Suddenly, his eyes lit up and he all but jumped up to his feet, knocking the stack of crates over behind him. "Wait a second," he said while looking over to Whiteoak. "You've got to have some more of that tonic in your wagon, right?"

Whiteoak froze like a rabbit that had just spotted the rifle pointed his way. "Well . . . yes, but—"

"I can pay you," Smitty said. The desperation in his voice was like a grating whine just beneath the surface. "It'll take all I got, but you can have it if I can just get another dose of that miracle tonic. Then all my problems will be solved."

Clint looked over at the professor, and swore for a moment that he could see devious wheels turning in his mind. Customers like these were what Whiteoak dreamed about. Clint wanted to jump in, but he decided to wait for a second to see if Whiteoak had changed any since the last time they'd met.

With his hands fidgeting at his sides, Whiteoak licked his lips as though he could taste the payday Smitty was offering. "How . . . how do you know it was my potion that had anything to do with what happened?"

Now Smitty stepped forward in a rush, gesturing excitedly as the words spilled out of him. "Because I could feel it! Sure as the day is long, I felt that firewater burn my throat and build me up into somethin' I always wished I was. I could feel my luck change that day! I swear I could feel it when it happened."

Whiteoak looked from Clint to Smitty, holding his hands out as though his mind simply couldn't handle the strain of what he needed to do. "Look," he said finally. "That tonic . . . it wasn't anything but water, laudanum, a shot of whiskey, and some molasses."

"But there had to be more than that," Smitty said. "I know there was, because it did more than just . . . it did what you said it would. There had to be something else in there."

"Actually there was." Now it was Whiteoak who shifted nervously on his feet. "There was also some salt."

As much as Clint had wanted the professor to come clean, he never truly expected Whiteoak to do so. Now that it was all out in the open, he waited in silence to see how the rest of it would play out.

Smitty started to say something several times, but always stopped himself before getting out more than a few sputtering syllables. "But . . . wait a second." Once again, his face lit up as he remembered something for him to cling to. "I shot Owen down. He drew on me and was gonna kill me, but I was fast enough to get the drop on him. How do you explain that?"

Whiteoak shrugged. "Lucky shot?"

For a second, Smitty stood just as still as the dust-covered bits of furniture strewn about the floor of the old store. Even his breathing seemed to stop. Clint could hear the sounds of rat's feet scurrying across the boards and the rustle of the wind shoving its way between cracks in the walls. And just when the silence began to take on a weight of its own, it was broken by the last thing Clint would have expected.

Laughter.

Smitty's shoulders jumped up and down. His stomach shook and his beard shifted on his face as the wide smile took over his mouth. At first, it sounded as though something was wrong with the old man's heart. His breathing became quick and shallow. He staggered back a step, and then let his body drop down onto the floor with a resounding thump.

Clint hurried over to his side, but moved back when he saw the partially hidden smile and the tears of laughter that formed in the corners of Smitty's eyes. Looking over at Whiteoak, Clint then shook his head and rolled his eyes.

"You mean to tell me," Smitty said through his frantic chuckling, "that my whole life got turned on its ear because of a lucky shot?" He looked up toward Whiteoak. "A goddamned lucky shot?"

"Maybe my potion helped you a little. You know . . . to loosen you up a bit?"

Climbing to his feet, Smitty wiped the tears from his eyes and walked up to Whiteoak. He then put his hand on the other man's shoulder and said, "Tell ya what, Professor . . . how about I try my luck again?"

Clint was moving just as soon as he heard what Smitty had said. Covering the distance between himself and Smitty with two bounding steps, he flashed out his hand to grab hold of Smitty's wrist just as the older man got a grip on his gun. There wasn't a lot of conviction in Smitty's attempted draw, but he did try to shake free of Clint's grasp.

"All right," Clint said firmly. "This has gone far enough."

Whiteoak didn't have a trace of fear on his face, or even so much as a hint of nervousness at having someone trying to pull a gun on him. Instead, he looked at the older man with tired resignation. There was something of a dare in the way he tilted his head and squinted his eyes.

The grip around Smitty's wrist tightened until the old man

finally let go of his gun. He didn't turn away from Whiteoak, but simply stared defiantly into the man's eyes until the professor finally backed down.

"You see what you did, Smitty?" Clint asked. "Right there, you turned him away because you got fired up enough to stop backing down when people cross you. Sounds to me like that's what happened with Owen. He pushed you so far until you just wouldn't let yourself be pushed anymore."

Smitty turned away from Whiteoak to look at Clint. "But ain't I still responsible for them that Lee hurt because of that damn body outside?"

"The only one responsible for that is Lee. Most towns would have had their lawman come in and put a stop to this nonsense long ago, but Chester doesn't have any real law. And that's not your fault either."

The anger drained out of Smitty's face, and was replaced by the quiet manner from before. "Then I want to help you put this right. I heard things while I was hidin' and tryin' to watch what was going on in town."

Exasperated, Clint said, "Go home, Smitty. And try to keep out of sight until this blows over. I don't want you getting hurt."

"And I don't want you getting hurt either," Smitty said. "That's why you should know about them gunmen that are coming in from Grand Junction."

TWENTY-FOUR

The men from Grand Junction were not hired guns. They wore pistols on their belts and had rifles strapped to the sides of their horses, but they didn't make their money from seeing other men killed. They were businessmen. And sometimes in business, other men had to come out on the bottom of a deal. Bottom could mean at the short end of a split, or it could be six feet below the soil.

They rode down through Utah, only stopping once to make sure their gear was ready and to discuss strategy. The one who spoke for them all was named Jarrett. A slender man, he'd been leading others for the last ten of his thirty-two years on earth. It was something he was good at. It was something he enjoyed. It was something to justify the harshness in his manner and the force he used to such lethal effect when there was no other option left open to him.

Jarrett could see the town of Chester drawing closer with every passing second. The fact that he had been forced to come here at all made his guts twist into an angry knot. Things shouldn't have gotten so far out of control. But things didn't always work out the way they were supposed to.

He knew it, but he didn't have to like it.

Jarrett was just a businessman. But the way he felt the moment he and his men rode into Chester, he was ready to do some shooting for free.

• • •

After sending his deputies out on their rounds, Sheriff Kenrick went back into the short hallway behind his office and stood in front of the two end cells. He twirled a large ring of keys around his extended finger and waited until Lee Respit responded to the noise.

Trying to keep calm as he swung his feet off the uncomfortable cot, Lee got to his feet and turned around. At the first sight of the sheriff, he charged the bars like a rabid dog, his hands flying between the steel to make a clumsy grab for Kenrick's face.

"Get me out of this damn cell before I pull you through these bars," Lee hissed. When the sheriff didn't respond, he grabbed hold of the cell door and rattled it with all his strength. "I said open this now, goddammit!"

Kenrick watched with a bemused look on his face until the other man lost his steam. "You done?" the sheriff asked.

In the next cell over, Nickolas Respit cringed and buried his face in his hands. He knew what was coming, and since it was usually directed at him, he braced himself for his brother's next tirade.

As predictable as always, Lee threw himself into a frenzied rage and slammed himself against the bars as though he fully expected them to give way. The door clanged against its hinges and the latch pounded against the lock, but in the end, steel won out over flesh and Lee staggered back with sweat pouring down his face.

"How about now?" Kenrick asked in the same even tone. "You done now?"

Lee spat on the ground and rubbed his shoulder. "What do you mean by locking us in here? This wasn't part of the deal."

"And neither was letting my deputies in on our arrangement, which is what I would have had to do if I let you go. So I suggest that you find a way to calm yourself down before I decide to keep you locked up all night."

"You can't do that. We both need to get to work or we lose our cut of that money." Sidling up to the cell door, Lee pressed his forehead against the cold steel and grinned like a hungry cat. "Or maybe I'll find my own way out of here and keep all the money myself. After spending some time in here, maybe I decided I don't want you for a partner no more."

The keys dangled from Kenrick's hand, swaying gently back and forth on their copper ring. "Jesus Christ, Lee, you two have only been in those cells for an hour or two. The way you're carrying on, you'd think that this was your first time inside one of those."

He stepped over to Nickolas's cell and fit the key into the lock. Turning it, he swung the door open on squeaky hinges. "Seems like your little brother here is taking it a lot better than you."

Even as the door swung wide open, Nickolas stayed on his cot with his knees drawn up close to his chest. He started to move, but froze and looked over to Lee before the soles of his boots touched the floor.

Lee glanced over toward the younger Respit and shooed at him with a waving hand. "Well, go on. We've wasted enough time as it is. Don't waste any more."

Only then did Nickolas get up and walk out of the cell. He pressed his back against the brick wall and shoved his hands inside his pants pockets, waiting for Lee to join him on the outside.

Kenrick took his time in finding the right key, which turned out to be the same one he'd used to unlock Nickolas's cell. He deliberately fumbled with the lock, and then pulled the door open, allowing Lee to step out into the open. Stretching his arms and rubbing his neck, Lee waited until the door was closed again before spinning the sheriff around and burying a fist into his stomach.

"That's what you get for fuckin' with us," Lee sneered. "*Now* I'm done."

The sheriff took in a deep breath and straightened up. An angry wince crossed over his face, but quickly passed away. "Good. Then let's get back to business. The others will be here any moment and we'd best be ready for them."

TWENTY-FIVE

"What men are coming from Grand Junction?" Clint asked.

Smitty turned his back on Whiteoak, pretending that he and Clint were the only two men in the room. "It's just like I said. I've been hiding out ever since Lee said he was out to kill me, and I figured the best way for me to stay alive was to keep tabs on where the Respits were. I lived in Chester a long time, and I know every nook and cranny in this town.

"Other day, I heard Lee talking to someone about these men coming in from Grand Junction and that they would start shooting the hell out of this place if'n they didn't get whatever they came for."

"What are they coming for?"

"I'll give you one guess," Whiteoak said from the back of the room.

Clint turned toward the sound of Whiteoak's voice, and found him kneeling over what appeared to be a square board that used to be part of the floor. Whiteoak had himself positioned so that he could pull the board up and set it to one side.

"What have you got there?" Clint asked. He walked over to where Whiteoak was crouching and looked down at the floor.

The trapdoor was only about two feet square, and led

106

down into a black space. From where Clint was, he could tell the compartment had been dug out of the earth and lined with old plywood boards.

"How far down does it go?" Clint asked.

Whiteoak looked into the dirty pit. "Far enough to hide in if you're desperate enough." He shifted on the balls of his feet until he could look straight down into the darkness. "And before you ask . . . yes, I was desperate enough once or twice."

"Does it lead anywhere?"

"Just down. It used to connect up to some old tunnel used for storage, but it must've caved in by now." Looking around the room, Whiteoak spotted something on one of the nearby walls, and walked toward the counter. Hanging from a hook behind the mildewed pile of lumber was a lantern. The glass was smeared with black grime and the base was completely covered with rust.

Smitty watched this from his spot in the middle of the room. He hadn't moved an inch since his laughing fit, but now he shuffled over to hunker down next to Clint. Peering down the hole, he whistled softly. "I never knew about that."

"I'm not surprised," Whiteoak said as he returned, shaking the lantern. "There's only been a dozen people who knew about that. Five of 'em are either in town or on their way."

"What about the rest?"

Whiteoak rooted around for a while, and eventually came across a box of matches. He struck one, lifted the dirty glass from the lantern, and touched the flame to its wick. "The rest are in holes just like this one spread out all over the country." The wick sputtered and sparked before finally allowing the flame to ignite. "Only difference is, nobody knows where those holes are."

"You said it was deep enough to hide in?" Clint asked.

Nodding, Whiteoak stared down into the hole as though he was waiting for someone to stick their head out and say hello. "It's not an easy fit by a long shot, but it's possible."

"Well, then, since you're the one that's been down there before, maybe you can try it again."

Clint's words hung in the air for a few seconds until they finally sunk in. When they did, Whiteoak snapped his head up and nearly jumped a step back. "Oh, no. I can't get down there . . . well, I could, but I . . . I just can't. I'm afraid of tight spaces. What about Smitty? He looks much trimmer than—"

"Smitty's got at least twenty pounds on you," Clint said while he grabbed hold of Whiteoak's sleeve and kept him from getting away. "You're the slimmest one of us, and besides . . . you know your way down there better than anyone."

"It's a damn hole, Adams. There is no *way* around there."

"Then consider this part of your sentence for coming into town and cheating poor Smitty here out of his money and the past few days of his life."

Surprisingly enough, the last part of that sentence seemed to have an effect on the professor. Whiteoak looked at Clint and then at Smitty. When he saw the old man standing there quietly, he took a deep breath and twisted around to break the hold Clint had on him. Whiteoak slapped his hands together and rubbed them vigorously as though he was warming them over a fire.

"All right," he said. "But the only reason I'm doing this is because this is why I came to this pisshole of a town to begin with." He then looked around the room to get his bearings. Finally, Whiteoak pointed to a corner adjacent to the front door. "There's a rope over there, stashed away beneath some of that rubbish. Could someone get it for me?"

Clint looked suspiciously at Whiteoak. "How do you know there's a rope?"

"Because I put it there when I first came to town. Jesus, Adams, are you always this jittery?"

"Smitty, could you check out that corner?" Clint asked. When the old man went over to look, Clint made sure he didn't take his eyes away from Whiteoak for a second.

After a few moments of rooting around in the piles of various garbage and leftovers, Smitty reached behind a stack of broken shelves and pulled something out. "He wasn't lyin'. I found it."

Clint still didn't look away from the professor as the old man came back and handed Clint a coil of rope that was too clean to have been sitting in its corner for very long. He

wrapped one end around his waist and handed the other end
to Whiteoak. After a few nervous sighs, the professor looped
the rope around his wrist and sat down at the edge of the
hole, dangling his legs into the darkness.

Whiteoak moved his toes around the inside of the opening,
and seemed to find a place that would support him as he
lowered himself down. He repeated that process, finding toe-
holds and shimmying down a little further. All the while,
Clint and Smitty could hear the professor's breaths coming
quicker, and eventually growing more and more muffled as
his head went below ground level.

"You all right down there?" Clint asked as the rope
snapped taut and then suddenly went slack in his hands.

At first there was no reply. Then, the sound of a hacking
cough came from the pit, followed by a scratchy voice. "I'm
fine," Whiteoak replied. "All this damn dust is playing hell
with my lungs, though. I'm at the bottom. Lower down the
lantern."

Clint pulled the rope up, and Smitty tied the end around
the handle of the old lantern that Whiteoak had lit earlier.
As the light was lowered down into the pit, Clint could see
the edges were lined with a skeletal wooden frame that had
been bolted to the sides with what looked like railroad spikes.
The planks were mildewed and blackened with so much dirt
that they all but disappeared against the dark background of
mud. The frame was in the vague semblance of a ladder
stuck to the sides. In a pinch, Clint figured a man could work
his way back up the hole on his own, but not if there was
anyone waiting up top for him with a gun in his hand.

As the lantern went further down, Clint could see the hole
widening out. He'd been concentrating so hard on looking
at the hole itself, that Clint was a little startled when Whiteoak's face suddenly appeared in the bobbing sphere of light.

The professor reached up for the handle and undid the knot
holding the lantern to the rope. "Okay," he called up to the
top. "Give me a second."

Clint was surprised to see the light move about a foot to
the side, and then disappear in what must have been a tunnel
that branched out from the bottom of the hole. He watched

for a few seconds, judging the depth to the bottom to be somewhere around twenty feet or so. The light began to dim and the sounds of Whiteoak's scraping steps became even more muffled. The tunnel down below was larger than what Clint had thought, however, and the light finally became nothing more than a barely visible glow.

"Whiteoak?" Clint called into the hole. "What are you doing down there?"

He waited for a few seconds, but could hear no response. Suddenly, he got a sinking feeling in the pit of his stomach, and began scrambling to find another lantern.

Having been staring down the hole while lying on his stomach, Smitty jumped to his feet. "Where'd he go?"

"I don't know, but I should never have trusted him."

"That looked just like a hole," Smitty said in disbelief. "I never even heard of a tunnel down there. I thought it was just some old well or something."

"Me too. If I thought he could get out of my sight, I never would've let him go down there," Clint grumbled as he searched the area where the first lantern had been. He spotted another lantern, and quickly got it lit. "Why in God's name did I even begin to trust that skunk?"

Clint had just stepped to the edge of the hole when another sound caught his attention. First, there was the sound of voices coming from outside the front door. Before he could hear enough to recognize any of them, Clint saw the door explode inward to reveal the snarling face of Lee Respit.

"I'll be damned," Lee grunted as he rushed inside.

There was another man on his heels, and another behind that one, both flowing in like a wave of humanity. Next through the door was Nickolas Respit, who was all but shoved inside at the end of a shotgun barrel. And behind that barrel was another grinning face that looked nothing like the first time Clint had seen it.

"Wrong place," Sheriff Kenrick said evenly. "Wrong time."

The sight of the silver badge on the man's chest caused Clint to pause half a second longer than he should have before drawing his gun. Although it was less time than it took to blink an eye, Clint's instincts told him that was enough to tip the scales in Kenrick's favor.

Rather than try to draw while standing in front of a shotgun, Clint did the first thing that came to mind. He held his arms in close to his body and ignored the heat of the lantern against his chest as he jumped feet-first into the dark, open pit.

TWENTY-SIX

The shotgun blast ignited the air above Clint's head as he felt himself starting to plummet feet-first into empty air. He was well inside the hole when the tip of his boot caught one of the planks fastened to the side of the wall. His toe snagged against the old lumber, causing the rest of his body to twist in midair, smashing his back against the damp earth. Pain shot up and down his spine when his backbone impacted against the edge of another wooden plank bolted onto the opposite side. His legs twisted painfully beneath him, but Clint managed to tense his muscles before both of his knees were bent in the wrong direction.

The sight of the room above was burnt into Clint's mind like a photograph taken at the moment the shotgun went off. Exploding gunpowder acted as the flash, freezing the entire scene perfectly. He could see the Respits standing on either side of the door, allowing the sheriff to walk inside and fire. He could also see the figure of Smitty Evanston in the corner of his mind's eye, dropping flat to his stomach with his arms covering the top of his head.

It wasn't Clint's way to leave someone in a pinch like that, but then again, he also knew that if he'd stayed up there he would have been dead inside of a second. Still, as the pain of straining muscles, hyperextended joints, and bruised bones pounded through his body, Clint almost thought about climbing back up to make sure Smitty was going to be all right.

Another shotgun blast from up top made him drop that idea like a hot rock.

The lantern was starting to burn his arms and chest where Clint was holding it. When he managed to get hold of it by the handle, he reached up and gripped the rusty metal strip between his teeth while trying to get a better hold on the splintered boards running down the length of the pit.

"Might as well come out of there, Adams," Sheriff Kenrick yelled from above. "We just want to talk some things over with you."

Clint knew better than to even dignify that with a response. Every part of him was on fire with its own kind of pain, but he used the fire within his body to keep himself moving. Taking a quick look below him, he saw that he'd wedged himself about halfway down the hole and there was another ten or fifteen feet left until the bottom. He wanted to move his foot down and step onto the next piece of lumber below him, but another surge of white-hot pain shot through his leg with a wave that, once it had passed, left him numb below the waist.

His teeth clamped down hard on the lantern's handle and his hands flailed to get ahold of something . . . anything . . . before he dropped the rest of the way down.

There were footsteps getting closer to the top of the hole, and Clint knew he heard the unmistakable sound of a shotgun barrel snapping shut after being reloaded.

"Just stick yer head out," said Lee's voice from the room over Clint's head. "We got somethin' to say to ya."

The lantern swung back and forth slightly as Clint shook his head. How he'd ever thought something involving Henry Whiteoak could turn out good was beyond him. That last attempt had dropped him another couple of feet, and when he could feel the footsteps getting closer to the top of the hole, Clint steeled himself and pulled his body off the wall to let it drop.

Planks rushed by as he fell, scraping against Clint's back like blunt, jagged claws. He made sure to tuck his head in close to his chest, and somehow managed to keep the back of his head from smacking against the side. His instincts alone got his legs to move so that they caught him somewhat once he finally hit the bottom.

For a second, Clint thought he'd landed on his feet. Then it felt as though the hole was being tilted and he dropped over to land painfully on his ribs. The lantern rattled his teeth, and would have knocked some out if he hadn't let go of it at the last second. His legs were tingling as though he was being stung by thousands of cold needles, but the sound of activity from the top got him scrambling for what looked like a narrow tunnel branching off from where he'd landed.

Clint threw himself headfirst into the tunnel, shoving himself along the ground like a panicked inchworm. He was just able to get onto his hands and knees and scramble forward as the next blast from the shotgun thundered down the hole.

Lead slapped into the ground, followed by a shower of wood splinters and chunks of dirt littering the spot Clint had just managed to evacuate.

Suddenly, a hand shot out from the darkness and grabbed hold of Clint's shoulder. Dragging him by the grip he had on Clint's shirt, Whiteoak pulled the other man deeper into the cramped passage.

"What's—" Clint started to say, but was cut off by a dirty hand pressed against his mouth.

For a few moments, the only thing breaking the silence was the occasional piece of rubble dropping to the ground after being shaken loose by the gunfire. Whiteoak reached forward and twisted the knob on the side of his own lantern. The light faded away until there was just enough left to show the vague outlines of both men.

"I guess this didn't cave in after all," Whiteoak said quietly. "Are you all right?"

Clint shifted around until he could get his feet beneath him. Every move he made was accompanied by a jolt of pain, but he could indeed move, and that was something to be thankful for. "I'm pretty banged up," Clint whispered, "but I don't think anything's broken." He looked around, but couldn't see much of his surroundings. "What is this place? I thought you said there was just enough room for a man to hide down here."

"Well, you may feel at home in here, but this space feels like it's closing in on me. Even with Kenrick up there, I'm thinking about crawling out of this damned grave." Whiteoak shuffled further back into the tunnel, helping Clint along the way. "What about Smitty? Did they . . . ?"

Clint winced at the grating pain that shot through both legs. There was definitely something wrong with his ankle, and his knees felt as though they'd been worked over with a sledgehammer. "I didn't get a chance to check on him before I dropped down here. They seemed to be shooting at *me,* though, so he should be all right for now."

"Yeah, sure," Whiteoak grunted. "Better hope that Lee doesn't catch sight of him before the sheriff does."

Even though Clint knew he didn't have much of a choice in what he'd done, he still felt bad about leaving Smitty to the Respits and Sheriff Kenrick. And when he thought about it a little more . . . he felt even worse.

"You'd be dead too if you were still up there," Whiteoak said as though reading Clint's mind. "Believe me, I know. All we can do right now is make sure we don't get killed. We'll worry about Smitty later."

Clint started to protest, but another blast from the shotgun made up his mind for him. The tunnel was just big enough for him to stand up with his back hunched over, which didn't do a thing to help the pain coursing through his body. He followed Whiteoak down the tunnel, listening to the sounds of someone beginning to climb down after them.

TWENTY-SEVEN

A nine-year-old boy dashed through the streets on legs energized with the power of youth and the promise of a silver dollar. The kid wore a wide grin as though it had been smeared across his face like a streak of grape jam. His breath came in short bursts and his arms pumped wildly at his sides.

He nearly bowled over an elderly couple making their way toward Mil's for dinner, and shouted an apology over his shoulder. He dodged in between a group of cattle drivers walking the saddle cramps out of their legs, and didn't even bother listening to the drunken curses they shouted at him after he'd passed. He rounded a corner and when he got in sight of the River's Lodge hotel, he added an extra burst of speed that threw him through the door like a cannonball.

"Slow down there, boy," the man behind the desk scolded. "What's the hurry?"

"Miss . . . Miss Tate," the kid wheezed in between gasps. "Where's Miss Tate?"

"Up in her room, but . . ."

The kid was gone before hearing the rest of the sentence, and was soon pounding up the stairs, making enough noise to wake up people in the other hotel across town. After a few seconds and three near-falls, the boy was in front of Room Number Six and was beating on the door with his fist.

Having heard the kid coming a mile away, Emily straightened her dress and was at the door before the boy could smash it in with his anxious knocking. She'd spent the last few hours making her initial rounds and getting a feel for the situation in Chester. Fatigue from the trip and the day's events was just beginning to set in before this little fish had come back.

Opening the door, she looked down at the boy with a gentle, motherly smile. "Back so soon, Matthew?"

"Yea, ma'am," the boy said while snapping to attention. "I waited right where you told me and saw those men ride into town, so I came and got you just like you said."

"How many men were there?"

Matthew was breathing so heavily that he had to shut his mouth, take a loud gulp of air, and swallow it before continuing. "Fi . . . five, ma'am. There were five of 'em."

"Did you get a look at them?"

"Yes, Miss Tate. They was all on horseback and was wearing guns. They dressed in nice clothes and didn't look like no cowboys. One of 'em was real skinny and looked mean."

Emily nodded. She could feel her heart beating faster and her own energy flooding back into her body as though she was being infected by the excited kid. Reaching into a small bag sitting on a table near the door, she pulled out a silver dollar and held it in front of Matthew just as she had when she'd offered him the job as her lookout.

"You did a fine job," she said. "Here you go."

Just as the boy was about to snatch the dollar from her hand, Emily pulled it out of his reach and bent at the knees to put her face at his level. "Just one more thing," she said. "Did you tell anyone about the job I gave you?"

Matthew shook his head without hesitation. "No, ma'am. I didn't want any of the bigger kids to take my money."

"Good thinking. You've earned your pay." Dropping the coin into Matthew's hand, she stood up and reached back into her bag. When she knelt back down again, she dropped a fifty-cent piece on top of the dollar. "That's a bonus because you're such a good boy. Also, I don't want you to tell anyone about me or that I wanted to know when those men got into town. Understand?"

Matthew nodded his head so vigorously that his mop of hair flopped down to cover his eyes.

"Now, where were they headed?"

After stashing his newfound fortune in his sock, Matthew leaned forward and whispered conspiratorially, "Four of 'em went straight to the sheriff's office. The other rode over to get a room at the Stone House Inn."

Plans swirled in Emily's head, and she nearly forgot about Matthew before closing the door. Stopping just before she left the kid in the hall, Emily opened the door a crack and said, "Keep your ears and eyes open. If you see anything strange, come and tell me about it and I'll take good care of you."

"Yes, ma'am!"

"Now scoot."

Once again, the hallway exploded with the sound of little feet pounding against the floorboards as Matthew all but threw himself down the stairs and out of the hotel.

Jarrett stepped inside the office of Sheriff Kenrick as though he was about to sit in the lawman's desk and prop his feet up. Instead of seeing Kenrick, however, Jarrett saw only the surprised faces of two deputies not even in their thirties.

"Where's Kenrick?" Jarrett asked.

One of the deputies was standing next to the desk at a narrow cabinet that contained a rack of rifles and ammunition. He quickly shut the cabinet and twisted a key in its lock before replying. "Just who the hell are you?"

Jarrett paid no mind to the other deputy, and walked right up to stand toe-to-toe with the one locking up the rifles. "I'm the man that just asked you a question, boy," he said with enough venom in his voice to make the younger man forget about the badge pinned to his shirt. "Now answer it before I get impatient."

The second deputy in the office had just closed the door leading to the jail cells, and his hand went immediately for the revolver that was strapped to his hip. Before he could clear leather, all three of the men accompanying Jarrett had drawn and thumbed back their hammers in a single fluid motion.

Letting the tension peak within the room, Jarrett waited a few seconds before taking a step back and motioning to his men. "We're not here to cause any trouble."

At their boss's command, Jarrett's men lowered their guns, but did not put them back in their holsters. Neither of the two deputies made so much as a flinch toward their own weapons.

"The sheriff's . . . not here right now," the deputy next to the rifle cabinet said. "I don't—"

From the door to the jail, the second law officer interrupted with. "He's out dealing with some prisoners. Why don't you put your guns away and we'll wait for him."

Nodding, Jarrett said, "Now I can see which of you two has the brains." Turning sharply on his heels, he put a hand on the shoulders of one of his men. "He'll stay here and wait while me and the rest of my boys get a room for the night. We'll be back to check in later." He stared directly into the eyes of the one he was leaving behind. "One hour."

Jarrett knew, without having to say anything else, that his man would come find him no matter where he was if he didn't come back in an hour. Deputies or not, Jarrett thought of that man as money in the bank.

Feeling some of his courage return, the deputy near the rifle cabinet squared his shoulders and took up a solid stance. "But you can't just barge in here and—"

"Settle down, boy," Jarrett said over his shoulder. "You can bluster all you want to my friend here. And don't worry . . . I'll tell Kenrick what a good job you did when I catch up to him."

TWENTY-EIGHT

"Someone's coming down here," Whiteoak said as he grabbed hold of one of the large nails that had been used to secure the wooden lattice to the walls. The nail must have fallen from the loosened soil.

Clint was taking a moment to get his wits about him after the beating he'd sustained from the fall.

Suddenly, a pair of boots slammed against the ground. Moving quick as a flicker, Whiteoak snapped his wrist and sent what looked like a rusty railroad spike past Clint's head and into the arm of Nickolas Respit.

Nickolas didn't even get a chance to draw his weapon before the spike landed solidly in his flesh. A pained howl came from his mouth and he pushed himself against the wall of the pit. Voices came from over Nickolas's head, and in the next second, another pair of boots landed in front of him. Lee was more prepared than his brother and already had his gun out.

There were still some cobwebs in Clint's head, but not so many that he was helpless when he was on the wrong end of a pistol. Although his hand wasn't as fast as normal, it was plenty quick enough to draw his modified Colt and take a shot at Lee.

Between the cramped quarters and awkward angle of the shot, Clint's bullet only managed to take a bite out of Lee's ribs. The gunshot resonated through the small tunnel, making the Colt sound more like a cannon as smoke and sparks blasted from Clint's barrel. A spray of blood popped from Lee's side, and the big man was spun around until he was facing the opposite direction.

"Does this lead anywhere?" Clint asked. "And don't bullshit me this time, Whiteoak."

"Just come this way," Whiteoak answered. His voice sounded distant and hollow, echoing from somewhere far behind where Clint stood.

Taking a quick glance over his shoulder, Clint saw the light from Whiteoak's lantern a good thirty feet down the cramped tunnel. From what he could tell, the professor was in a small room and was still moving deeper into hiding. Clint backed his way down the hall, making sure he was ready if either of the Respits decided to come in after him.

Lee snarled like a wounded bear as he wheeled around to fire in Clint's direction. When the smoke billowed toward him, Clint remembered the shotgun and knew that if that was coming at him again, he'd be dead where he stood.

But the weapon in Lee's fist was a pistol. And though it could have killed him just the same, the gun only fired one round rather than a barrage of them. That one round blazed halfway down the tunnel and dug itself deeply into the earthen wall, stopping just short of Clint's body.

"All right, Adams," Whiteoak said from even farther away. "We've got what we came for, so let's get the hell out of here."

Clint was having a hard time seeing much through the combination of gun smoke and dust that had been kicked up from the flying lead. Still making his way backward down the hall, he was ready for anything to come through the dirty haze, and when something did, he sent a round through the dust and quickened his pace into the next room.

The bullet from Clint's gun cut a narrow path through the grit hanging in the air. Lee's chest had just pushed through when the shot came. Clint couldn't be sure if he'd hit much of anything or not, but his shot served its purpose in that it caused Lee to back off immediately.

After a few more hurried steps, Clint realized he was no

longer in a tunnel, but in some kind of dimly lit chamber. The mouth of the tunnel was framed with the same kind of wooden latticework that lined the pit and walls. Old mildewed beams crisscrossed the interior like a lumber skeleton. The room was only about ten feet square, but seemed like a wide-open space compared to the tunnel he'd just left behind.

The light in the room was coming from a single source, which bobbed about at the end of Whiteoak's outstretched arm. The professor held the lantern as he rushed up to Clint's side, nearly causing Clint to take a shot at him out of pure reflex.

"What the hell are you—" But Clint stopped his question when he saw Whiteoak reach out and grab hold of a solid-looking door open next to the tunnel's entrance.

"Stand back," Whiteoak said as he gave the door a shove.

Clint did just that, and was barely able to avoid getting smacked in the back by the moving slab of wood. The door fit snugly into its wooden frame, giving an ominous thud as it crashed into place. Before the sound could fade away, Whiteoak had set the lantern down and was busy straining to pick up a piece of lumber that was easily three inches thick and four feet long.

The sound of hurried footsteps could just barely be heard on the other side of the door. Clint holstered his gun and grabbed the other end of the lumber, which was giving Whiteoak no small amount of trouble. Between the two of them, they were able to lift the heavy piece of wood and drop it down into a set of brackets bolted to either side of the door.

When the footsteps drew closer, Clint and Whiteoak stood back and watched as the door shook within the frame and dust billowed out from between each piece of wood. Lee's muffled voice seeped through the door, but neither of the men could make out any specific words. When the big man on the other side tried one more time to ram the door, the thick piece of timber held tight.

"That should hold even if the sheriff brings that shotgun down here," Whiteoak said between labored breaths.

Clint stood, ready to draw if that door came bursting inward. But the only thing that seemed to be in any danger of breaking was whatever part of Lee's body was pounding against the wood. The noise stopped for a moment, and Clint took a second to look around the chamber.

There wasn't much that he'd missed the first time he'd surveyed the small room, except for the small stacks of crates piled up in three of the four corners.

It was only now that Clint spotted the small box tucked away securely under Whiteoak's right arm. The way the professor held on to it, that box might have contained something that was alive and defenseless. But before Clint worried about that, there were other more pressing concerns to deal with.

"So are we trapped in here?" Clint asked.

Whiteoak turned and headed for the back of the room. Once the lantern was closer to it, the entrance to a second tunnel could be seen as a gaping black maw cut into the rear wall. "No, but we could've been out of this damn hole if you hadn't stopped for target practice."

Clint followed the professor out of the room and into the adjoining tunnel. This passage was even more cramped than the one they'd left behind. "You're right," he said to Whiteoak's back. "Next time I'll just let whoever it is take their shots at you and step over the body. Or better yet, I'll blindly follow you and get a bullet in my back."

For a change, Whiteoak was silent as he made his way through the darkness. Clint could hear the man's breathing becoming shallower and faster. It was understandable since the further along they went, the more the ceiling dropped and the closer the walls drew in to their sides. Eventually, they walked single file, shuffling in a low stoop-backed crouch and holding their hands balled up in front of their chests.

Clint felt as though every breath he took sucked the life from the little bit of stagnant air that was in this place. Thoughts began running through his mind, making him feel as though he was being led to a suffocating end in the murky blackness, or that Whiteoak would turn around at any moment and take a shot at him. Or maybe he would simply fall over when his lungs were unable to pull in another breath.

After a few minutes that felt like the better part of a day, Whiteoak stopped and set the lantern down in front of him.

Clint couldn't make out much of what the man was doing, but in a few seconds, he could hear the sound of a latch sliding into place, and then a dim light drifted into the tunnel.

Whiteoak had to hunker down even lower to get through the small door, and once he was through he stepped to one side and let his body drop down to sit against a wall. Following in Whiteoak's footsteps, Clint managed to squeeze through the opening, which led into what appeared to be a storm cellar.

"Before you ask," Whiteoak said while pushing the box he'd been carrying toward Clint's feet, "that's what Kenrick and Lee would've been after."

As much as Clint wanted to vent his anger and frustrations out on Whiteoak, he decided to wait until he got a look inside the box. The container was the size of a thin shoe box. It had obviously been well cared for before it was buried beneath the streets of Chester. The wood was sanded down to a smooth texture, and despite the layers of dirt and grit on its surface, the box still retained some of its polished finery.

There was a small key in a keyhole, both made of rusted copper, embedded in the front of the container. Clint turned the key, and the box opened easily. Its interior was lined with dark red felt, which made the large uncut diamonds look all the more brilliant when they caught what little light there was in the cellar.

"Jesus Christ," Clint said in a low, awed voice. He tilted the box in his hands, watching as the diamonds shifted about on the soft felt, giving way to yet another layer of smaller gemstones. Besides the diamonds, there were several pebble-sized emeralds and the occasional nugget of gold. "What is . . . ? How much . . . ?" Clint stammered. Finally, after closing the box, all he could get out was another "Jesus Christ."

"Yeah," Whiteoak said evenly. "My thoughts exactly."

TWENTY-NINE

When Jarrett stepped into his room at the Stone House Inn, he drew his gun and took aim before his eyes got a chance to completely focus on the woman sitting on his bed. Even when he did realize who it was, he didn't holster his gun right away.

"You still like playing around with dyin', Emily?" he sneered after shutting the door behind him.

Emily Tate sat perched on the edge of a smallish mattress that was covered with a soft, quilted comforter. Both hands were resting on the blanket, and her back was arched just enough to push her large breasts forward. She wore nothing but a short black slip and boots that laced up to just below her knees. Her legs were crossed, and her reddish-blond hair spilled over both shoulders.

"You remember me well enough," she said. "I'm never one to turn down anything that'll make my heart beat a little faster."

With that, she uncrossed her legs and set both feet on the floor. The slip was the perfect length to give Jarrett a quick glimpse of what was underneath. There was a flash of skin, a hint of blond hair between her legs, and then she was on her feet walking toward him.

"What the hell are you doing here?" Jarrett asked.

Emily waited until she was close enough to slip her arms

around his neck and lift herself up on her toes. "Same thing as you," she whispered into his ear. "Claiming what's mine and seeing that the one who took it from me gets his due."

"You don't have the first notion of why I'm here."

"Of course I do." She was pressing her body against him now, circling around him until the butt of his gun rubbed against her stomach. "If we work together, think how much faster we can be done with all this." Emily's hands drifted to his crotch. She cupped his penis through his pants and held him firmly. "Then we'll have time to play. I remember what you like," she said while squeezing a little harder.

Jarrett suppressed the desire that was threatening to overtake his reason. His hands moved through her hair and over her shoulders, tracing down her sides as his thumbs brushed over the sides of her breasts. "If you're here for the same reason as I am, then you should know how much I'd gain by just killing you." He kept his hands moving until they rested on her deliciously plump backside. "That would be one less person to split the money with."

Emily had her eyes closed and was rubbing herself against Jarrett's revolver. She wriggled within his hands and reached up to run her hands over his chest. "You could kill me, but I don't think you will. You couldn't in Santa Fe, so why should you now?"

"There's a whole lot more at stake now."

"And there's so much more to gain."

Even as her hands went to work on him, Jarrett kept his face straight and his voice steady. "Santa Fe was different."

"You're right," she said. "In Santa Fe we had to make do with a pool table and five minutes of privacy." Maneuvering herself back onto the bed, she crawled up onto the mattress and leaned forward to grab hold of the pillows, raising her backside into the air like a cat in heat. "Here we've got this room and all the time we need."

Jarrett started to move forward so he could get his hands on her, thinking he was going to toss her off the bed and out of his room. He knew that she was trying to get on his good side any way she could, and he'd be damned if he was going to let himself be such an easy target for her manipulations.

On the other hand, he couldn't deny for an instant that the

way her body was sprawled over his bed was making his own muscles twitch in anticipation of touching her again. That thin, filmy slip clung to her body as she pressed her chest to the bed and reached out with both hands, causing the material to slide down the curve of her buttocks and gather at her waist. The mound of blond hair between her thighs poked out invitingly, framing soft, moist lips. Jarrett held on to his self-control right up to the moment when she reached back and pressed her finger into that glistening tuft of hair to spread it apart, showing him the soft pink creases beneath.

Before he knew what he was doing, Jarrett was tearing his clothes off and grabbing hold of her from behind. His rod was so hard that it had begun to ache, but relief came the instant he plunged it inside those beautiful pink folds and grabbed hold of that plump backside with both hands.

Emily seemed surprised with how fast he was upon her, and clawed at the bed with both hands until she got ahold of a pillow and buried her face into it. She let out a scream into the pillow as he entered her. The sound of flesh slapping against flesh filled the room, soon to be followed by the sound of Jarrett's hand smacking the side of her buttocks.

She whipped her head back and let out an almost animal grunt as he kept pounding deeper inside her. Emily's voice became hoarse and scratchy after only a few minutes, and she started crawling forward until she disengaged from him. Once she got to the head of the bed, she lay down flat on her stomach and held her hands behind her back.

Jarrett remembered that well enough from last time, and knew exactly what she wanted him to do. Holding her by the waist, he propped her up just enough for him to penetrate her again from behind, before grabbing hold of her wrists with one hand. As he pushed his hard cock inside, he took hold of her by the hair and pulled her head back just until another delighted cry came from Emily's mouth.

"God, yes," she said. "Do it hard, just like I like it."

Hips thrusting with every ounce of strength he could muster, Jarrett slammed into her and watched as her plump backside jiggled with every impact. The sight of it made him harder, which made him want to fuck her even more. When his own grunts of pleasure started getting louder, Emily wriggled out from under him and started rolling over onto her back.

She got up and hopped down off the bed, making her way to the washbasin. Her naked body was wet with perspiration and red from where Jarrett's hand had smacked her skin. She loved the feel of the warm spots on her buttocks, and loved even more the tingling heat between her legs.

Once she was at the washbasin, Emily dipped her hand into the cool liquid and splashed it down her chest. Her nipples hardened immediately and her stomach clenched from the shocking cold. When she turned around, Jarrett was already on his way to her, his stiff cock pointing the way.

"We're not done yet," he said.

Emily sat on the edge of the small table and spread her legs. "I know."

Her sex was slick with moisture, and when she reached down to pull her sensitive lips apart, her blond patch of hair was split down the middle by a strip of pink. Jarrett's cock nudged against her opening, and he worked it in with a few pushes of his hips. Before he did any more, however, he reached down, lifted her up, and walked until her back was pressed against a wall.

His strong arms held her there, and Emily wrapped her legs around Jarrett's waist. When he began pumping into her, she raked her nails down his back and screamed as every muscle in her body began to tingle.

Sweat ran down Jarrett's face, over his shoulders, and down his back. He strained and pushed into her. All he could feel was her warm wetness, and all he could hear was her voice crying out for more. Finally, a wave of pleasure shot through his system, giving him the strength to pump into her one last time.

Emily had angled her hips so that her most sensitive areas were rubbing against his shaft. As his thrusts became stronger, she grabbed onto him as though he was the only thing keeping her from flying away. And when he pushed inside her that one last time, a fire started where their bodies joined and raged through her body, igniting her from her toes to the top of her head. It was still surging through her when he carried her back to the bed and set her down.

He dropped next to her. Neither of them was able to move for the next few minutes. When they got enough strength to crawl beneath the covers, they lay side by side, neither one willing to drift off to sleep.

"This isn't going to change my mind," Jarrett said as he stared up at the ceiling. "I'm still going after that money . . . all of it."

"What are you going to do with twenty-five thousand dollars?" she asked.

"I'll think of something."

Emily rolled over, pretending to be upset by what he'd said. Once she knew he couldn't see her face, she allowed a smile to play across her lips, and had to fight to keep from giggling just a little. Now she was certain that Jarrett really didn't know about how much was actually hidden away beneath the town of Chester. Allowing Jarrett to find twenty-five thousand of it was a fair enough price to be rid of him and his men. Especially when there was easily ten times that much to be found.

And as for the sex . . . she'd enjoyed it as much as any woman. But mainly, after years of dealing with men like Jarrett, she'd found that they always felt more in control after they'd had their way with a woman.

All the better, she thought. Feeling in control and being in control were two very different things.

THIRTY

Clint stared at the box full of glittering gems as though he was transfixed. He'd seen a lot in his time that men would kill for. Everything from gold to stacks of money and even fine jewelry, but none of it quite compared to what was now right in front of him. What he was looking at would have been enough for him to retire and live comfortably for the rest of his life. And he could probably take along a good part of Chester with him as well.

"Where did all that come from?" Clint asked, suddenly feeling very nervous to be around so much unclaimed wealth.

Whiteoak turned the box around so he could take a good look himself. "Remember those mines I told you about? Well, most of it came from those, and the rest came from other folks who stored it away for safekeeping and forgot to make their withdrawal before getting themselves killed."

"Killed how?"

"Take a look at this again, Adams. Most men don't have to think too hard before they come up with a way to kill whoever's holding something like this."

"Why didn't you tell me about this to begin with? Before, you just said Respit and some others were after the deeds to those mines, not a fortune in jewels."

Whiteoak closed the box and tucked it under his arm as though it was his newborn child. He then began to nervously

130

pace about the room. After giving the place a quick once-over, he walked up to Clint and whispered, "Because not everyone knows about this. Sure, they know that there's a fortune buried in those properties, and most of the properties are mines.

"Just about everyone looking for me thinks that it's the mines themselves that are so valuable. I made sure of that when I found out about it a few months ago, and it makes a helluva lot of sense to keep it that way."

Nodding, Clint said, "I'll bet. That way, even if someone gets those deeds from you, you can always sneak in later to grab the gold or whatever is in there." Suddenly, Clint's face dropped. "So, you mean to tell me that there's more boxes like those in other towns?"

"Yeah, but none worth this much. The rest is mostly gold and silver. This is the most valuable stash . . . not to mention the easiest to carry."

Clint walked toward the other end of the room. It appeared as though they were in a cellar. Although it obviously wasn't abandoned like the parts they'd left behind, this place didn't see a lot of use either. "Where are we?" he asked.

Whiteoak was standing in front of the opening that led back into the tunnel. With one hand, he pulled something that appeared to be a large wooden frame away from the wall. That frame was actually hinged to the wall, and closed over the tunnel entrance. The front of the frame looked like a set of empty shelves, and when it was in place, there was no way of knowing what lay behind it.

"We're in a cellar within the town limits," Whiteoak said. "I only heard about it on the day before I got here, and never got much of a chance to look into it before I was arrested." He walked across the room again and pressed his ear to a closed door opposite the fake shelves. "It sounds like there's plenty of people up there."

Clint walked up to the door and listened for himself. Sure enough, he could hear quite a few voices in various conversations. He couldn't recognize any of them, but then again he couldn't hear much above a murmur anyway. At the very least, none of the voices sounded hostile.

"Okay, Whiteoak," he said, standing between the professor

and the door. "Before I take another step into this, I'm going to have to insist on one thing."

"You can take my word, Adams. I don't have any other weapons on me."

"That's not what I meant." Reaching out, Clint tapped the box under Whiteoak's arm and then held his own hand palm up. "Give it over."

Whiteoak's whole body seemed to close in around that box, and he reflexively took a few steps back. As he got closer to the shelves, the sounds of muffled gunfire could barely be heard in the tunnel beyond it. Apparently, someone was blasting away at the locked underground chamber with the shotgun.

"You can't be serious," Whiteoak said. "I nearly got killed for this so many times that I've lost count. I came all this way . . . went through so many contacts and tracked down so many leads . . . all so I could just hand this over to you?"

"I thought you trusted me. Or at least, you seemed to trust me with protecting that miserable hide of yours."

"And I thought you tr . . ." Whiteoak knew better than to finish that sentence. "Why do you want me to hand it over?"

"Because I don't trust you," Clint stated. "I've got no way of knowing if you're telling the truth about where all that came from. For all I know, that's the biggest load of stolen jewels I've ever seen in my life." Listening to the sounds of distant gunfire rumbling through the connecting tunnel, Clint shook his head slowly and crossed his arms. "I'd say you haven't got too much longer before that shelf there comes crashing down."

For a second, Whiteoak looked as though he was going to hold his ground. Then, with a labored sigh and a dramatic gesture, he presented the box to Clint and glared like a man possessed as it was taken from him.

"I'm no thief, Whiteoak. If I find out that you have rightful claim to any of this, I'll gladly hand it over. But until then, I'm keeping it." The box felt heavy in Clint's hand. The weight reminded him of just how much wealth was inside that polished wooden container. Honestly, he felt like he was carrying a powder keg, and was already thinking of a place where he could dump it.

"Can we go now?" Whiteoak asked. "Or are you going to stand there with that smug look on your face?"

Clint stepped aside and let Whiteoak go ahead of him. The professor stepped up to the door and slowly opened it to reveal a narrow staircase leading to another door that stood ajar at the top of the stairs. Not wasting another moment inside the cellar, Whiteoak began climbing the stairs, with Clint directly behind him, until they were both at the top.

Whiteoak tested the doorknob, and found it to be unlocked. Slowly twisting the tarnished metal handle, he opened the door and climbed the last remaining stair. When they emerged from the stairway, they found themselves in a large, well-lit room with people bustling back and forth and rows of cabinets and tabletops. Along one side, there was a long, narrow window that opened onto another room. Next to that window was a door, and on the opposite wall was a pair of large black stoves.

Clint immediately felt the heat from the stoves when the door opened. Then he got a whiff of something that made him certain of where he was. Stepping around Whiteoak, Clint looked at the rest of the room. Most of the people were busy enough that they didn't notice the two new arrivals right away. There was one who saw them plainly enough, however.

"How long have you been down there, Clint?" Sam asked with a genuinely shocked expression on his face.

The smell alone had been enough to make Clint think of Mil's. Seeing the portly Indian cook standing there with his hands stuck inside a plucked chicken was more than enough to prove him right.

THIRTY-ONE

The shotgun roared in Sheriff Kenrick's hand one last time before he stepped away from the door to let Lee Respit kick at it some more. The cramped tunnel was still shaking from the last few times the gun had gone off, and the air was thick with black smoke. No matter how brittle the door looked, the timbers simply would not budge under Lee's boot. All the shotgun had done was manage to take a few chunks out of the wood itself.

Exasperated, Kenrick said, "Give it up, Lee. There's something wedged in there and we're not gonna get it out from here."

Lee's breathing was heavy enough after climbing down the hole, shuffling down this length of corridor, and now kicking at the unmoving wooden barrier. He put both hands on his knees and took a few much-needed breaths. Before he spoke, he hacked up some of the grit that had gotten into his lungs and spat it onto the packed dirt. "They're probably trapped in there anyways. Why not just get some dynamite and bury them inside? We can dig up the rest later."

Kenrick was already making his way back to the bottom of the hole that had brought them this far. "That's a real good idea. I'm sure that they just locked themselves in there without any way to get out."

"Well, I never heard of any other way besides—"

134

Kenrick wheeled around on Lee, forcing the other man to take a few steps back. The sheriff's normally placid face was contorted with rage, and he clutched the shotgun in front of him as though he was about to pull the trigger or just shove it down Lee's throat.

"This whole damn thing is about mines, you dumb son of a bitch! This might be a small one, but there ain't no mine that goes for ten or twenty feet and then just stops.

"That there is a small part of something that runs beneath a good part of this whole town," the sheriff said while jabbing a finger over Lee's shoulder toward the bolted door. "So you can bust your foot on that piece of wood until it breaks off, but I'm not staying down here one more minute when those two bastards could be anywhere else at this moment. Hell, they're probably out and on their way out of town by now, thanks to you."

Now it was Lee's turn to feel the anger rake through him like a cold winter wind. His hand fumbled for his gun and when he drew the pistol, the business end of the sheriff's shotgun was already poking him in the chest.

"You go ahead and do it," Kenrick snarled. "Then I'll only have one brainless Respit in this town to worry about."

Even though he was one muscle's twitch away from getting his lungs blown out through his spinal cord, Lee actually seemed to take a moment to contemplate firing his pistol. His eyes didn't lose a bit of their fire before he eased the gun back into its holster.

Kenrick pushed Lee toward the end of the tunnel, where Nickolas was waiting with his back pressed up against the wall. The sheriff tested the rope he'd tied off to one of the planks bolted at the top of the hole. Satisfied that it would hold his weight, Kenrick used it to work his way back up into the abandoned store.

He went to the back of the room and knelt down so he could look into the eyes of Smitty Evanston. Smitty's wrists were manacled. The old man's body hadn't stopped shaking for the entire time that Clint had been gone, and when he saw the sheriff approaching, he closed his eyes and waited for the gunshot that would end his life.

"I ain't going to kill you, Smitty," Kenrick said with disgust tainting his voice.

That seemed to ease the other man's nerves a little bit, but not enough to keep him from shaking. "Th . . . then someone else will . . . whenever you turn your back on him. Lee wants to kill me."

"What for? You think he's still mad about losing Owen?"

Now the shakes took hold of Smitty again as the sound of Lee climbing up from the pit reached his ears. "Please," he whimpered, "don't let him kill me. I swear I was only defendin' myself."

By this time, Lee was out of the hole and stomping toward the spot where Kenrick and Smitty were talking. He jerked the pistol from its holster and walked over until the barrel was less than an inch from Smitty's forehead.

"You gonna try'n stop me, Sheriff?" he asked after thumbing the hammer back.

Kenrick stood up and stepped aside. "I told you once before, I don't give a shit if this old fool lives or dies. That was part of our deal."

A crooked smile snaked its way over the corners of Lee's mouth. He let out a gust of foul breath and started squeezing his trigger.

"But you might want to think about one thing before you do that," the sheriff continued. "Now that Clint Adams is in the picture, you might want to think about getting yourself some insurance."

Lee's eyes narrowed and he glanced over toward Kenrick. "What the hell you talkin' about?"

"Just that Smitty here was with Adams when we found them. Looked to me like they were getting along pretty good. Kill him now, and he'll be after you for murder. Hell, I'm still the law in this town. Kill him in front of me and I might have to bring you in if things come down to it."

"Then turn your back."

"Gladly. But if Smitty's alive, he could serve a purpose . . . at least until we get our hands on that money. He might even make things easier on us. After that . . . who gives a shit what happens?"

Lee thought about that for a few seconds, and then moved

the pistol away from Smitty's face. "Keep talking."

Behind them, Nickolas was just pulling himself out of the pit. He dropped down heavily onto the ground, and nearly fell all the way down to the bottom of the narrow shaft. He saw the two men huddled around the cowering figure of his brother's killer, and automatically went for his gun.

Nickolas had only drawn the old Smith and Wesson twice before, and neither time had been against another human being. But this time, he felt he couldn't do anything else. One thing for sure. He couldn't stand by and watch as Lee and Sheriff Kenrick bartered for the old bastard's life. "Stand aside," he said as he pointed his gun toward Smitty Evanston.

Lee's head perked up and he took a glimpse behind him. "Is that you, Nicky?"

"Yeah, it is. Now stand aside and let me take care of this if you ain't gonna. That old man's gotta pay for what he done. There ain't nothin' else he's good for. If you ain't ready to settle this, than I guess it's gotta be me."

"Sure, Nicky, sure," Lee said as he turned and started stepping aside.

Before Smitty was able to draw a bead, Lee's gun fired once and sent a bullet straight through Nickolas's chest. The younger Respit dropped to the ground with a look of stark surprise on his face.

"I call the shots in this family," Lee said as he walked over and kicked the gun out of Nickolas's hand. "If you had an ounce of brains in yer head, you would've learned that already."

He stood there and watched the light fade out of his brother's eyes. Then he turned back to the sheriff. "Sorry you had to see that," he said with a shrug toward Nickolas. "Family business."

THIRTY-TWO

"Where's Mandy?" Clint asked Sam once the cook led him and Whiteoak outside Mil's kitchen and into the dining room.

"She's staying at my home," the cook replied. "Isn't that where you wanted her to wait for you?"

Clint nodded, and tried to look as inconspicuous as possible as he walked from the kitchen into the middle of a dinner crowd. There was an older couple paying for their meal just outside the kitchen door who gave him and the professor curious looks, but other than that, most of the other folks were too busy with their meals to be bothered by whoever was coming or going from the kitchen.

Whiteoak was taking losing possession of the box of gemstones better than Clint had expected, which meant only one of two things. Either the professor was biding his time and waiting for a perfect moment to try to take it back, or he actually didn't mind passing the hot potato off to someone else who might have an easier time with the next set of people who came gunning for it.

Clint really didn't care which it was, so long as he was able to keep an eye on Whiteoak at all times. When they were outside the restaurant, the cook rattled off directions to his home.

"Did anyone come looking for her?" Clint asked.

Sam shook his head. "Not that I know of. But I had to be at work most of the time anyway."

"Has anyone ever mentioned anything about the cellar in that place? Or have you even heard rumors about anything connected to that building?"

"Not really. Does that have anything to do with how you two got down there without me or anyone else noticing you?"

"Yeah," Clint said. "It does."

At first, Clint thought he'd walked into the wrong place. The spare key had been stashed away beneath the corner of a woven Navajo print rug just as Sam had described. The building was the one he'd pointed out. The number on the door was the right one, but once Clint stepped inside, he had to take a moment and check everything again just to be sure.

"Good Lord," Whiteoak said as he pushed past Clint and walked inside. "If this is how the cooks of the world live, then maybe I'm in the wrong line of work."

The furniture in the place was sparse, but it was all made of finely polished oak and cedar. Two chairs were covered with stitched pads that looked like something more comfortable than Clint had sat on in months. A cedar chest in a corner was carved with scenes depicting wildlife around a large brass lock, which looked as though it would have taken several shots from any firearm to get it open without a key. A small bed in the back of the room resembled something from an expensive hotel. Its posts reached nearly to the ceiling, and the mattress was covered with a layer of soft, inviting blankets.

"And I thought Indians were supposed to live simply," Whiteoak grunted.

Clint walked further inside, and noticed that there was a small, closet-sized door set behind a painted wooden screen. "Most don't have much of a choice in the matter," he pointed out. "But this is a little . . ."

"Extravagant? I'd say. Especially for a cook's wages."

Clint walked to the small door and gave it a few sharp raps. "Mandy? Are you in there?"

At first, there was no noise from the other room. But just

as he was about to knock again and try the door's handle, Clint heard light footsteps padding closer from the other side. The door swung open, and Mandy was standing there with a worried expression on her face. Her cheeks were flushed red and her hair was sticking out at odd angles. As soon as she saw Clint, she ran into his arms and held him as tight as she could.

"Oh, Clint, I'm so glad you're all right," she said. "All I've been doing since I got here is thinking about what could be happening to you and if maybe Lee might have tried something terrible. . . ." Her voice trailed off as she rubbed her hands over his back. That simple action seemed to soothe her nerves, and she eventually pulled away. That was when she noticed the wooden box under his arm.

"What's that?" she asked.

"Better if you didn't know just yet," Clint replied. "Has anyone else come looking for you?"

She shook her head. "No. Everything's been pretty quiet since I got here."

"Does anyone else know you're here? Or did anyone see you when you arrived?"

"I didn't tell anyone besides Sam . . . just like you told me. I tried to be as quiet as I could. On the way over, I passed a few folks, but I waited until they were gone before I went inside." Another look of concern darkened her features. "Is everything all right? What happened while you were gone?"

Clint took a look inside the second room, and found it to be a small guest room. There was a simpler bed, a dresser, and not much else. Walking over to a narrow window, Clint made sure to keep himself mostly behind the thick black curtains as he scanned the street outside. Besides the occasional passersby making their way from one boardwalk to another, there was nobody to be seen. "It's a long story," he said without taking his eyes from the street. "As long as you're safe here, I think it's best that this is where you stay."

"Oh, no," she said. Mandy's voice was sharp and resolute. "I tried sitting around and waiting for things to happen, and I didn't like it one bit. Also, I'm not too fond of having a bully like Lee Respit kick me out of my own home."

"It's for your own protection, Mandy. I can't be every-where at once."

"I know, and nobody expects you to be. All I'm saying is that if you need me, I'll be at my place, where I can at least get a change of clothes."

Clint didn't like this at all, but he could tell from the woman's voice that nothing he would say was going to make a bit of difference. Turning on his heels, Clint walked from the room. "Fine. Do what you want. If you need me, I've got a feeling that I won't be hard to find. Just listen for the shooting."

THIRTY-THREE

By the time Jarrett met up with all but one of his men and made his way to the abandoned storefront, the shadows were creeping over the body of Owen Respit, making it look like a lumpy pile of rags in the street.

Jarrett didn't give the corpse a second glance. He'd seen enough dead men in his time, and he knew he'd be seeing plenty more. His first look had told him who the young man was and what had happened to him. As for the specifics . . . well, he was a businessman after all, and his business lay inside the deserted building.

Stopping outside the storefront, Jarrett waved one of his men forward with a casual gesture. "Go check on Cal," he said. "Make sure he's taken care of everything and then come back here. This shouldn't require more than three of us."

"Yes, sir," the other man said. He took off down the boardwalk at a quick pace, and disappeared around the corner within a few seconds.

Jarrett drew his gun and took a quick look at his men to make sure they were ready. The two others with him were dressed in black suits, which made them look like gamblers or landowners. The only thing setting them apart from one another was the weapons they carried.

Jarrett had his .45 in hand, while the man next to him brandished an Army Colt. The remaining figure held a Spencer rifle over his shoulder, and nodded that he was set to go when Jarrett looked his way. Just as the group's leader was about to open the door, he stopped and flicked his hand quickly to the side.

Immediately, all three men scattered away from the door just as chips of wood blew outward and the sound of muffled gunshots exploded from inside the store. They crouched down low, Jarrett heading around the building while the other two took up positions beneath windows on either side.

As one, the two near the windows stood up and began pumping rounds through the dirty glass, even as lead started to whip by their heads and chew apart the frames.

Jarrett was heading toward a side entrance, and when he got there, he sent his boot crashing through a boarded-up door. The rotted wood gave way easily, and when he entered, Jarrett saw two familiar faces, one stranger, and another dead Respit.

"Hello, Kenrick," Jarrett said as he squeezed off a round at the sheriff's feet.

The lawman was crouching down low and scuttling for cover as bullets rained in from the outside. His eyes darted over toward Jarrett, but his body kept moving for cover behind the dusty counter at the back of the room. Once he was safely behind the solid wooden barrier, Kenrick glared at Jarrett, the finger on his trigger visibly twitching with anticipation.

"Hold your fire," Kenrick shouted. Then, to Jarrett, he said, "It's about time you showed. I'd have thought you and your men would've been here a lot earlier. As it is, you're too late to do much of anything here, unless it's just me you're after."

Lee had been ready to put a bullet into Jarrett's chest before he heard the sheriff's order and saw who it was. By now, the front door was open, and the black-clad man with the Colt came striding through, leveling his pistol at Lee.

"What do you mean we're too late?" Jarrett asked. His eyes darted toward the hole in the floor.

Kenrick slowly stood up and held his gun down at his side. "Whiteoak's come and gone already—and he had help this time. Someone calling himself Clint Adams, but I don't

see why a man like that would want to side with Whiteoak.
Everything I hear says that Adams don't take too kindly to
outlaws."

Still aiming at the sheriff, Jarrett scowled as the thoughts
ran through his head. "Principles tend to fall by the wayside
when this much money gets involved."

Lee had been ready to kill or be killed when the shooting
just seemed to stop. He noticed as the second man walked
through the door that they were aiming at him, but not quite
ready to fire. Hearing the mention of money pulled Lee's
attention toward the conversation taking place at the back of
the room.

"And where did Whiteoak go?" Jarrett asked.

The sheriff nodded toward the hole. "Down there. Adams
jumped in as soon as we got here, leaving that one behind."

Smitty had been cowering in the corner farthest from the
front door the last time Kenrick had checked. Now, however,
there was no trace of the old man.

Jarrett started laughing. "Looks like another one got away
from you. Fine job you're doing here, Sheriff Kenrick. A
fine job indeed."

Kenrick was so mad that he was beginning to shake. Despite the guns in the room, he stormed over toward Jarrett
and stood toe-to-toe with the man in black. "If it was up to
me, none of this would've happened. We would have killed
Whiteoak in Santa Fe when we had him dead to rights."

"Sure," Jarrett said calmly. "And then we would have
never found out about this place. How long did you have the
deed to this establishment, Kenrick? Two . . . three years?
And you nearly sold it for a couple hundred dollars to some
saloon owner. And what about you, Lee?"

Jarrett motioned for his employee to lower his Spencer.
"How long ago was it that your father died and left you those
properties in California?"

"He didn't—" Lee started to say. But he quickly held his
tongue, and his eyes began nervously darting about the room.

Now Jarrett was smiling widely. "Ahhh, that's right. He
didn't leave them to you, did he? He left them to your brother
Owen." Jarrett walked past the sheriff and around the broken
counter until he was standing within ten feet of the hole and

about fifteen feet from Lee Respit. "I believe I ran into Owen outside. Or nearly ran over him, I should say. I must admit, I never thought you'd have the nerve to kill your own brother."

THIRTY-FOUR

Those words were enough to distract Kenrick from his anger. "You told me your father left you those deeds."

Lee became a cornered animal as he started taking steps in one direction, only to back up and try another. He couldn't quite seem to position himself so that he wasn't closer to one person or another. Jarrett and his men had slowly begun to close in on him, taking one cautious step after another.

Finally, Lee got his back pressed up against a wall, and he turned to look at the sheriff. "What difference does it make?" he shouted. "Everyone in town knows I didn't kill Owen."

"Oh, that's right," Jarrett said with a slight chuckle. "You made that painfully obvious, didn't you? And why didn't you kill whoever did it? I'm sure you've had plenty of opportunity. Or did you finally give up your violent ways?" With that, Jarrett snapped his gun toward Lee and thumbed back the hammer. Both of his men followed his lead and raised their weapons.

Almost instantaneously, Lee took up his pistol. It was pure survival instinct that kept him from pulling the trigger.

"Well," Jarrett said quietly while looking from Lee to the body of Nickolas Respit. "I guess you've got some of that instinct still in you after all."

At that moment, the front door opened. Only the man with

the rifle turned to look, while his partner kept his Colt trained on Lee. Jarrett also looked, but held his aim where it was.

Standing in the doorway, looking as though she'd just entered a social gathering held in her honor, was the woman all of the others had been waiting for. She wore a simple green dress that came all the way down to the heels of her brown leather boots. Matching ribbons tied her hair back into a lush, flowing tail. She clutched a handbag in front of her with one hand, and held a handkerchief up to her nose with the other. She stepped inside and shut the door.

"Why is it that we can never get together and work together civilly?" she asked.

Jarrett smiled and lowered his gun, as if in tribute to the lady's presence. "Because we are the only businesspeople here, Miss Premont. And we're forced to work with swine."

Taking away the handkerchief, Mandy Premont smiled curtly and stepped past the rifleman, positioning herself next to the man holding the Colt on Lee. "Wasn't it enough that you left that carcass outside for the entire next day after Owen was killed?" she asked Lee. "Didn't you think the whole town would get the point that it wasn't you that shot him?"

Ignoring Jarrett, Kenrick walked out from behind the counter. It wasn't until Jarrett's men swung their guns toward him that he realized he was still holding his weapon. He holstered it and looked from Mandy to Lee. "Then how'd you get Smitty to take the fall for you? Hell, there's more than a dozen folks in town who swear they saw him shoot Owen."

Lee clenched his mouth shut, the muscles on either side of his face tensing as his teeth gnashed together.

"Why not just tell him, Lee?" Mandy said with an amused tone playing at the edges of her voice. She watched him for a few tense seconds before it was obvious that Lee wasn't about to say another word. So she gladly took up the rest of the story. "Plenty of people saw Smitty shoot his gun, but not a one of them saw the bullet that did the job. And not a blessed one of them would have seen Lee picking off his brother from across the street." Turning toward Jarrett's man with the Spencer, she added, "Using a gun pretty much like that one."

"Why talk about all this now?" Lee grunted. "What the hell does this have to do with anything?"

This time, it was Jarrett who stepped forward. He glared down at Lee as though the other man wasn't anything more than a piece of filth he'd just scraped off the bottom of his boot. "We're addressing this because Miss Premont and I are businesspeople. Not wild dogs nipping at each other's heels. Before people can do business, they need to know who they're dealing with.

"And now that all our cards are on the table, I propose that we work together for once and put an end to this entire affair. If not for all this petty squabbling, we would have been splitting up our money long ago."

Sheriff Kenrick slowly turned toward Jarrett. "Then why don't we start by putting our guns away and going after Whiteoak instead of each other?"

"A good suggestion," Jarrett said. With a snap of his fingers, his two men lowered their weapons and stepped back to position themselves by either door.

"Now," Mandy said as she walked over to look down into the hole that gaped in the middle of the floor. "Has anyone else been down there?"

Kenrick spat on the floor and glared over at Lee. "We saw Whiteoak go down there before we came in. As soon as we busted through, Adams jumped in and they got away through the tunnel."

"And I suppose you lost their trail somewhere in the ten feet of passageway between there and the cellar?"

Anger flashed across Kenrick's face, but was tamed by a calm, deliberate breath. "No. By the time we got down there, they were ready for us. We chased them into a room and they closed the door. It's bolted from the inside, and it's too damn solid for us to get through unless we dynamite the damn thing."

"Which would make you the first volunteer to start digging out our money when the whole place caves in," Jarrett said pointedly.

"None of that will be necessary," Mandy said before Kenrick could unleash the profanities he had prepared for the businessman. "They already made it out and got their hands on what we're all looking for."

The sheriff looked about in confusion. "But we've been here this whole time!"

Mandy spoke to him as though she was explaining a simple lesson to a particularly stupid child. "The tunnel doesn't just go one way. It links up with another cellar, and I've made it my business to keep my eye on where it empties out just in case something like this happened.

"And now that it has, I can tell you that Adams and Whiteoak are indeed working together and that Adams is the one who's got our property." Mandy walked away from the hole and looked out through one of the shattered front windows. Bits of glass crunched beneath her feet.

All the aggression that had tainted the air like a gaseous fog seemed to have dissipated in the space of a few seconds. Every man in the room looked from one to another, either confirming their own positions or sizing up the threat the others posed. Jarrett slid his toe beneath the square trapdoor and flipped it over until it slammed shut on top of the dark pit. "There's not a lot left to do then," he said. "Since we all know where we stand, we should begin by—"

"Hold up for a minute now," Lee interrupted, catching the attention of every person in the room. "What about that bitch of yours? The one that's left behind more blood than any of us so far?"

Kenrick turned his head to watch the businessman's response.

Jarrett didn't so much as twitch an eyelash. "Emily's here. I'll tell her what happened and she'll do her part."

It was obvious that there was more to be said about this woman, but nobody in the room seemed willing to say any of it. For the time being, they all stayed quiet and mulled over the reminder that Lee had given them. Suddenly, the group began working their way from the middle of the room and toward the doors. It was as though something in the air told them that they'd been in one space for too long.

Mandy was first at the door. Her hand rested on the handle, and she was about to walk outside when she stopped, turned around, and spoke. "Now, then," she said, "if you fellas wouldn't mind waiting for just a little while longer before you go around shooting everything in sight, I may just be able to get this whole thing worked out even neater than we'd planned."

A sly little smile crept over her face as she thought about her dealings with Clint Adams. The way he'd spoken to her, confided in her, touched her, all of it was enough to convince Mandy that she'd done a perfect job of putting the famous man right where she'd wanted him. The notion of it made her body flush with excitement. Suddenly she wanted Adams inside her again, wanted him naked and loving her just so that she could see how perfectly she'd trained him.

"With a little luck," she added, "we might even get our property delivered to us by the great Gunsmith himself."

THIRTY-FIVE

Clint posted Whiteoak as a lookout in front of the sheriff's office while he took the box of gems they'd found and stored it away for safekeeping. Since he knew exactly where he was going, the trip took less than half an hour. Clint slipped from alley to alley under the cover of darkness, making his way back to where he'd left the professor.

Part of him wondered if Whiteoak would still be there when he got back. But although Whiteoak might very well be the least of several evils in Chester, he was still a thief first and foremost. And no thief worth his salt would ever consider the notion of skipping out on a payday as big as this one. Clint could only guess at the true value of those gems, but he was certain it was no small fortune.

It was a big one.

Whiteoak would still be there, all right. Of that, Clint was certain.

Sure enough, when he crept around a corner and ducked into an alley that cut between two quiet buildings, Clint could see the huddled figure of Henry Whiteoak waiting just where he was supposed to be. Clint rapped quietly on the side of one of the buildings and headed down the alley.

Hearing the sudden sound, Whiteoak twitched and spun around, his eyes visibly wide even with the sun long gone from the sky. "Where is it?" he asked after catching his breath.

Clint shook his head. "Not yet. I'll tell you that when this is over and when all the dust is settled. That is . . . if I decide you need to know at all once that happens." He looked toward the sheriff's office. "Anything been going on there?"

"Near as I could tell, there's only two deputies inside. I could see them walking past the windows. They looked more nervous than scared, which means that there's probably someone else in there with them."

"That's a good piece of deduction, Henry."

"Well, I also saw one other man in there through the window as well." He glanced behind him, and then back at the office. "It's one of Jarrett's men."

"And who's Jarrett?"

"Just the one man that got this whole mess started," Whiteoak said. Noticing the scowl etched across Clint's face, Whiteoak corrected himself. "Well, the one man besides me, that is. Jarrett is a bounty hunter who only takes private jobs from rich landowners and such."

"A gun for hire."

"Pretty much. But if you ever call him that to his face, you'd best already have your own gun drawn. He's the man who I met over cards some time ago. A damn fine player. He could palm an ace, slip it into the middle of a deck, and then throw it back into his own hand while you thought he was just scratching his nose. Anyway, he was good enough at first for me to think he was a straight player. And there ain't no professional gambler that can pass up a straight player."

Clint thought about all the cards he'd played in his lifetime. He loved a good poker game, and could even handle the fact that a lot of players cheated. But he had to agree with Whiteoak that there wasn't anything better than just sitting down to a deck of cards and betting on fate for a few hours. Unlike Whiteoak, Clint saw honest players as good companions rather than easy marks.

Shaking himself out of his own musings, Whiteoak continued. "Anyway, Jarrett thought he had me going all the way through a game that went through one day and halfway through the next. We traded a few good hands and between us, we managed to weed out every other player at the table. Finally, he lets me have those deeds as bait, figuring I'd get cocky and try to clean him out just like any other sucker would.

"But I knew better. I took my winnings, cashed out my chips, and said my good-byes." The smile on Whiteoak's face betrayed the fact that, even after all the trouble that had followed, he was still proud of that one shining moment. "And he's been after me ever since."

If Clint hadn't seen men nearly draw down on other gamblers who left without giving them another shot at winning their money back, he wouldn't have believed Whiteoak's explanation. But he had seen it. Plenty of times.

"Turns out that Jarrett has a little group he works with," Whiteoak said. "He figured getting ahold of my properties was important enough to get them together."

"Did you ever think that those weren't just one man's deeds you won?" Clint asked.

Whiteoak actually seemed to ponder that . . . for all of about two seconds. "No. I just put 'em in my pocket after winning them away from that man. If he didn't want me to have them, he shouldn't have dropped them onto the table. Soon after that, I heard about how valuable they truly were. And the rest . . . well, you know about the rest."

Clint was about to say something else when the door to the sheriff's office swung open and one of the deputies stepped outside. The youthful lawman with the badge on his chest waited in the door, looking at something further down the street. Turning to see for himself, Clint found that that something was actually a someone. A very attractive someone at that.

"Oh, shit," Whiteoak whispered as soon as he saw who the deputy was looking at.

From where he was, Clint could just see the profile of a voluptuous woman who knew how to show herself off when she walked. She wore an elegant black dress that was trimmed with red lace. The colors blended into the night like an oil painting, and even across the distance separating them, he could make out the generous curves of her breasts as well as the fine slope of her backside. Long, reddish-blond hair swept over the side of her face, hiding most of it from view.

"You know her?" Clint asked.

Whiteoak was reflexively going for where his gun should have been. When he found nothing at his side but empty pockets, he pushed himself deeper into the shadows. "Yeah, I know her, all right. Her name's Emily Tate. She was with Jarrett at that card game . . . and everywhere since then."

Clint watched as the attractive strawberry blonde walked up to the deputy and began talking to him in a voice that was too quiet to be heard from the alley. The deputy seemed to be more than happy to help her with whatever she was asking for, and he took a step out of the office. The woman took a quick glance over the young man's shoulder, and then walked close enough so she could take the deputy's arm. The lawman looked surprised at first, but then he walked her inside as though he was escorting her to a dance hall.

"So what's your problem with her?" Clint asked.

But Whiteoak was already pressed up against the wall. "Can't I just get that box and get the hell out of this town? I mean, that way all these brutes will just pack up and go after me." Whteoak's face brightened all of a sudden. "You might even say that I can clean up this town for you. And I swear to God you'll never hear about me again."

Ignoring the professor's babbling, Clint kept his eye on the sheriff's office. He didn't like the idea of a woman being in there whenever Kenrick and the Respits came back. And he sure didn't like the idea of her or the deputies being in the line of fire once the shooting started. "Just shut up, Whiteoak. I can't just turn my back on this. There's still Owen's murderer that needs to be dealt with."

"If you wanted to deal with Owen's murderer, why didn't you do it when Smitty was standing right next to you?"

"Because he didn't kill Owen," Clint said casually.

"What? How do you know?"

"I saw that body when I first came to town. That wound didn't look like it was done at close range. There weren't even any powder burns on his shirt. And I've met Smitty. I don't care what kind of potion you might have given that man. There's no way he shot Owen."

"So then who . . . ?"

"That's the question. And with Kenrick being what he is, that leaves us as the only ones interested in the truth around here. Well . . . one of us anyway."

Offended, Whiteoak put his hands on his hips and looked like he was about to stomp his foot. "You know something, Adams? I don't appreciate these constant remarks about my character. I'm a changed man. I've been doing my best to—"

Whiteoak's sentence was cut off by the sharp pop of a single small-caliber gunshot. If Chester had been a busier town, nobody outside the sheriff's office might have heard it. But the shot, although faint, was distinctive to Clint's ears.

Clint was halfway to the sheriff's office when he saw the door open and a deputy run outside and away down the street. Then the other deputy took a step outside. "You need some help in there?" Clint asked.

The deputy started to answer, but all he could manage was a wet cough. It was then that Clint saw the fresh bloodstain on the young man's chest.

THIRTY-SIX

Clint ran from the alley and headed straight for the sheriff's office. The young deputy took another staggering step, which nearly sent him pitching straight down as he fell from the boardwalk. Arriving just in time to catch the wounded man, Clint did his best to gently lower him to the ground.

"What happened?" Clint asked.

The deputy struggled to catch a breath. When he finally managed to pull some air into his lungs, he said, "Don't know . . . who . . . someone after the woman . . ."

But Clint knew better the instant he saw the fleeting glimpse of a figure standing in the office doorway. It was a man dressed in black. That man's gun was drawn, and as soon as he saw where the deputy had landed, he calmly stepped back inside.

Clint was up and charging into the office, determined not to let the shooter get away with gunning down a lawman who probably had no idea about what was really going on. He covered the space between the street and the door in two bounding steps. Kicking in the door with a swift boot, Clint ducked back around the door, expecting another volley of gunfire to come from the inside.

But that gunfire never came. Instead, all Clint could hear was the pounding of footsteps as they retreated further into the building. Clint was inside, and then face-to-face with the strawberry blonde he'd seen entering the office.

"Who are you?" Clint asked, remembering what the deputy had said about the woman. "Is someone after you?"

The woman appeared rattled, but not deliriously so. "I'm all right," she said breathlessly. "The deputy . . . is he . . . ?"

"He's outside." The only other door from the office that Clint could see led to the jail cells, and wouldn't have been his first choice for a getaway. "Where did he go?"

The woman pointed a shaky finger toward the jail. "In there," she whispered.

Clint stalked toward the door, took hold of the handle, and got ready to pull it open. He then looked at the woman, who was standing directly behind him. There was something he didn't like about this. Something was very wrong.

Just as he had outside, Clint took a quick step to the side of the door before he pulled it open. Reacting quicker than he'd seen most gunfighters move, the woman threw herself to the side before the door was fully open, narrowly avoiding the bullets that blasted from the hallway and into the office.

Clint caught a glimpse of her face. She wasn't panicked or scared. She wasn't acting on impulse or gut reflex. Her face was calm and calculating. Her expression betrayed more anger than surprise at Clint's maneuver. She'd known that those shots were coming and she was mad that they didn't hit him.

All of that registered in less than a second. In the next second, Clint's gun was drawn and firing through the door. Two holes appeared in the wood, followed by a pained grunt in the next room. After he heard the thump of a body hitting the floor, Clint looked back over to the woman . . . just in time to see the flash of skin as she flipped her skirts up and reached between her legs.

He'd seen enough written on her face to know that this woman was not just an innocent victim caught in a cross fire. Clint had also seen his fair share of dirty fighting tricks to recognize that the black garter strapped to her leg was there to hold a lot more than just her stockings.

While she reached to the inside of her thigh, Clint moved around the door and into the narrow hallway of cells, closing the door behind him. Slouched on the ground with his back propped up against the bars, the man in black gripped his rib cage with one hand, and reached desperately for the gun he'd dropped with the other.

"I'll save you the trouble," Clint said as he kicked the gun out of reach with one well-placed foot.

From the other room came the familiar sound of a gun. It was the same small-caliber pop that he'd heard from the alley, only this time it was loud enough for him to know it had come from a derringer. A small hole appeared in the door, followed by the shower of splinters falling in the bullet's wake. Clint thought about shooting through the door again, but two things held him back. He didn't like hurting women. And unless she'd reloaded the derringer, that was probably her last shot.

He tried not to think about the *unless* part as he opened the door and stepped back into the office.

Clint was ready to act in case he found himself staring at the wrong end of that little gun, but he let out his breath when he saw the office was empty, the front door still swinging on its hinges. "Damn," he said as he made his way to the window looking out to the street. When he peered through the glass, he saw only two figures outside. Neither of which was the one he was looking for.

"Where'd she go?" Clint asked.

Henry Whiteoak crouched down over the deputy and was examining the lawman's wound.

"She headed off that way," he said while pointing toward the nearest street corner. "And she had a gun in her hand. Didn't even stop to . . ."

Whiteoak didn't bother finishing his sentence because there was no longer anyone there to hear him.

Clint took off running for the corner, careful not to charge headlong into any kind of trap. Deciding to put his money on the poor accuracy of the derringer, Clint readied himself as he ran around the corner.

The street was deserted except for a few people strolling down the boardwalk. He walked halfway to the next corner, keeping on the alert for any trace of the woman, but found only shadows and curious bystanders. Suppressing a curse, Clint spun around and headed back to the sheriff's office.

THIRTY-SEVEN

By the time Clint made it back, Whiteoak was getting to his feet and brushing the dirt from his hands and knees. The deputy was lying just as Clint had left him, fresh blood glistening in the moonlight.

"Did you catch her?" Whiteoak asked.

"No, but I'll catch up to her soon enough. Now let's get that kid to a doctor." Clint walked to the deputy's side and started to bend down to get the young man moving, but Whiteoak stopped him with a hand on his shoulder.

"Don't bother, Adams. He's gone."

Looking down at the deputy's face, Clint knew that Whiteoak was right. The young man's body had the eerie stillness of the recently departed. The chest seemed sunken somehow. The arms and legs looked disconnected from the rest. Empty eyes stared blankly up at the sky, searching for that missing essence . . . or maybe just watching it leave.

Clint could feel anger boiling up inside him as he reached down and closed the deputy's eyelids. He was sick of seeing people roll through towns like these and trample innocents in the name of greed. He was sick of all the shady dealings that went on to bring about deaths like this, and most of all, he was sick of watching killers leave their victims rotting in the street as though they were nothing more than piles of garbage to be picked up later.

Whiteoak stood next to Clint, silently staring down at the body. "He was a good one, Adams. Even when I was brought in and thrown into that cell, this one treated me decently."

"Did he know about any of it?" Clint asked. "Did he know about the gems and the people coming after them?"

Whiteoak shook his head. "No. And that's the damned pity of it all. The funny thing is that most of the people after that money probably don't even know how much there is."

"What do you mean?"

"Just what I said. I dealt with Jarrett and his men a few times. Even met Lee and his brothers once or twice, but I don't think any of them ever saw all of what was down there."

"Let me guess," Clint said quietly. "You never told them where the entrance to the tunnels was."

"Nope. Just like I never told them exactly what it was they were looking for. They knew there was gold, but they didn't know squat about what we found."

"Is there gold?"

Nodding, Whiteoak said, "Oh, sure, there's gold. What do you think was in all those other boxes?"

Clint's mind was racing with plans and possibilities. He and Whiteoak moved the deputy's body into the office, and covered him up with one of the long coats hanging on a rack in the corner behind Kenrick's desk. Whiteoak was just about to leave when he stopped and tilted his head like a dog listening to a faraway whistle.

"There's someone back there," Whiteoak said while pointing toward the door leading to the jail cells.

Clint listened, and could also hear the sound of someone shuffling in the next room. "That would be the man I shot. I was just about to have a little talk with him."

When he opened the door, Clint could see the man in black stretched out in the middle of the hall, reaching for the gun that had been kicked away from him. Every movement brought a twinge of pain to his face. Each strain made the blood flow that much more from his wound.

"Jarrett must be paying you an awful lot to get this kind of devotion from his men," Clint said as he walked into the

hall. "Or are you just trying to finish the job before he fin-
ishes you instead?"

The other man went limp and let his arm drop to the
ground. When he rolled over onto his back, there was a dark
red stain on the floor as well as a small dagger in his fist.

"Fuck you," he grunted as the blade flashed from his hand.

There wasn't nearly enough strength in the throw to cause
Clint any worry, and the knife didn't even make a full turn
in the air before it clattered noisily against the bars of the
first cell. Clint took a few steps forward while shaking his
head. He bent down, retrieved the knife, and walked over to
stand between the man on the floor and the gun he was
crawling toward.

With one snap of his wrist, Clint sent the blade whipping
through the air. It dug into the floor less than a foot from
the wounded man's head with a solid thunk. "You want to
try again?" Clint asked. "Or would you rather talk to me
now and then we'll get a doctor? If we're lucky, we can get
that wound looked after before you bleed to death. If not . . .
well, I'm sure the fine sheriff of this town will do his best
to look into the circumstances of your death."

As much as the other man tried to keep up appearances,
it was obvious that Clint's words had an effect on him. He
didn't even try reaching for the knife. Instead, he pushed
himself back until he could sit up against the wall. His eyes
were already beginning to glaze over from the pain and loss
of blood. "We're not the killers here," he said between
spasms of pain. "Jarrett and the rest of us are here to claim
what's ours." Suddenly, his eyes seemed to light up, and he
raised a bloody hand to point toward the office. "That one . . .
he stole from us."

Clint looked over to notice that the man was pointing at
Henry Whiteoak, who was standing in the doorway. "I've
heard all this," Clint said impatiently. "Just tell me where
Jarrett and the others are."

"He wanted to look at the property and then . . . head out
to find that cheating swindler."

Seeing that he didn't have much time before the wounded
man passed out, Clint started getting him to his feet. "All
right. Now tell me who that woman was."

"Emily," he grunted as he was pulled upright. "Emily Tate. She said we were wasting time guarding deputies. She . . . shot one of them . . . said it was better not leave any witnesses. The other run off."

Rather than push the man any more, Clint helped him to one of the cells and laid him on a cot. Just then, another set of footsteps came rushing into the office. Clint spun around and nearly drew his gun before he saw who it was.

"I heard there were shots coming from here," Mandy said as she ran inside. "I had a bad feeling that it was you. With all these gunmen in town—"

"There's one man dead outside and another wounded in the jail," Clint said in a rush. "Get the doctor and be quick about it."

Mandy seemed as though she was either about to run or cry as she looked around the room to find a mess of blood on the floor. She chose the former, and rushed outside.

Clint was on his way out when Whiteoak hurried to catch up with him. "What now?" the professor asked.

"Now we find all the players and get together for one last hand. The chase for this damned money ends tonight."

THIRTY-EIGHT

Emily Tate hurried down an alley as though her heels were on fire. By the time she emerged from the other side, however, her walk was just as calm as those surrounding her, and she looked like just another lady out enjoying her evening. She headed for the casino, but stood outside and waited before going in. When she was confident that there was nobody to see her, she slipped away from the gaming hall and walked next door. The smell of burning opium and incense wafted beneath the door, and the sound of wind chimes lazily clinking against each other drifted on the breeze.

Hurrying inside, she was greeted by a thin Chinese man wearing a black shirt buttoned all the way to his neck. His hair was slicked back and braided in a long strand. Emily looked around, squinting in the paltry light given off by two lamps burning just bright enough to hold a flame.

"You want seat?" the Chinese man asked with a thick accent.

"Actually," Emily began, "I think I see who I want from here."

Her eyes had locked onto a figure sitting with his back pressed up against the corner in the farthest alcove of the cluttered room. Rugs covered the floor, and pillows were piled up in stacks all around. On those stacks were the reclining bodies of well over a dozen people, mostly men, who

163

were either passed out or too overcome by the smoke they
were inhaling to move much more than their lips around the
pipe.

The Chinese man stepped in front of Emily as she began
to walk toward that figure in the back. "You no bother," he
said in a hasty whisper. "I take message."

"Leave her be," said the man in the back.

The Chinese man stepped aside and bowed apologetically.
Emily strutted over the intoxicated patrons like a princess
walking among lepers.

"God help me, but I always liked this place," she said
while fluffing a few pillows and lowering herself down onto
the floor. "Although I'm surprised you still come here. I
mean after being elected sheriff and all."

Kenrick chuckled softly. He placed the metal tube to his
lips, pulled in a deep inhale, and let the smoke curl around
inside his skull. "Soon I won't need this badge anymore."
His words came out slowly and deliberately, each one an
effort in concentration. "I'll be rich enough to buy this town
and make myself the mayor."

That brought smiles to both of their faces, and when he
tried to laugh, a stream of thick smoke came out instead.
Emily gathered her legs beneath her and waved her hand
toward the Chinese man who'd met her at the door. Almost
immediately, there was a pipe prepared and placed in her
hands.

She puffed on the copper tube, not allowing the fumes to
venture too far. For Kenrick's benefit, she closed her eyes
and breathed in deeply through her nose. After holding the
smoke in her mouth for a second, she pursed her lips and
blew it out. "Mmmm," she purred. "I like it."

"Give it another minute," Kenrick said after leaning his
head back and closing his eyes. "It'll get better."

Despite the cool air outside, the inside of the opium den
was heated by a potbellied stove sitting against one wall. The
odor of sweat was heavy in the air. Emily mimicked the
sheriff's motions, and pretended to be affected by the opium
she'd never inhaled. In reality, as she moved slowly back
and forth, she let her wandering eyes take in the layout of
the room. She watched where the Chinese attendants were

walking and how they made sure not to intrude upon their customers' privacy. She counted the unconscious bodies sprawled out on pillows, and noticed a man and woman savoring their pipes while slowly writhing in each other's arms.

Then she got an idea.

Pressing herself tightly against Kenrick's side, Emily draped one of her legs across his lap and rubbed it up and down. With every move she made, the dress crept even higher up along her thigh. She held the pipe between her fingers, running the cool metal down the sheriff's chest. His shirt was unbuttoned down to his stomach, and a few probing fingers opened it the rest of the way.

"What're you doing?" Kenrick asked.

Emily feigned a slur. "Making it feel better. You want me to stop?"

"What about Jarrett?"

"He's not here right now, is he? But you are. And I want to take advantage of this sensation while it's still fresh inside me."

Emily's hand brushed over Sheriff Kenrick's chest, teasing his skin and scratching down his ribs with the tips of her fingernails. The way his eyes were glazed over and staring off at some distant point, it was unclear which he was enjoying more, her touch or the opium.

Taking him by the wrist, Emily moved the sheriff's palm over her leg and pressed it firmly onto her backside. She moved on top of him, reaching her hand between his legs. She cupped him in her hand and massaged his cock until it began to harden. An even bigger smile drifted across her face as Emily worked his pants open and felt inside.

The fog was clearing from behind his eyes as his body began to respond to Emily's touch. She had his cock in both hands and had pulled it free of his clothing. It stood erect in front of her, and she rubbed its length with quickening strokes.

Leaning forward, Kenrick grabbed Emily by the back of the head and drew her closer to him. Their lips met in a fierce kiss. Her tongue probed inside his mouth, teasing his lips, while she continued to handle his pole. Without breaking their kiss, the sheriff started pulling her dress down to

her waist, exposing her breasts to the dim light of flickering
lanterns.

She moved her shoulders to help his clumsy hands, reaching up to pull his shirt open all the way. When she began
tugging at his pants, Emily straddled Kenrick's hips, enjoying the feel of him between her legs. She was still wearing
her lacy stockings, but there was nothing else beneath that
skirt besides herself and the garter holster.

Kenrick's hands moved up and down her body, freely exploring the curves of her breasts and the slope of her back.
He moved her clothes aside when they were in the way, but
didn't bother taking the dress completely off her. In fact, he
ran his hands beneath the material gathered at her waist, savoring the contrast between it and her creamy skin. When
he looked around, the others in the room were either too
engrossed in their own activities or respectfully turning their
eyes away.

Just as the sheriff's hands were drifting toward the derringer, Emily reached down and pulled them back up to her
breasts. She pressed them against her, leaned her head back,
and shifted her hips until she could feel his manhood sliding
between her legs. With a few squirms in the right direction,
she impaled herself upon his hard shaft and lowered her body
down on top of him. Emily let his hands go, knowing full
well that they would stay right where she'd put them. She
reached down to gather up her skirts, and held them in front
of her so she was free to move as she pleased.

Her rounded backside clenched and shook as she bounced
on top of him. The smoke swirled about her head, giving her
a sample of the pleasant mental tickle of the opium. Kenrick's hands squeezed her breasts and then clamped onto her
bottom, guiding her thrusts as she quickened her pace.

They were both moaning quietly, not caring about the others in the room or why any of this was happening. Even
though she was enjoying the feel of the man inside her, the
smile on Emily's face was not brought about by that pleasure. Instead, it was a response to how easy it was to get the
town's law to lie down and expose himself for her.

A little giggle formed at the back of Emily's throat, which
Kenrick thought he had created. He flicked his thumbs across

the base of her spine, tickling the upper slope of her buttocks in an attempt to get another one of those giggles. When he was finally able to open his eyes all the way, the sheriff saw a vision straight from a dream rising high above him.

Emily's full, rounded body bounced deliciously as he pumped his cock up into her. Her nipples were like little pieces of hard candy framed perfectly by her wavy locks of hair. She ground her body on his, rubbing against him until she hit just the right spot, which sent chills of pleasure through her entire body. Holding the back of the sheriff's head, she pushed him to her neck and breathed heavily as he started to nibble on her skin.

Her legs clenched tightly around him, and both of their hips were thrusting against each other with increasing speed and ferocity. Their moans turned into grunts, and those became louder each time he buried himself deep between her legs. Emily could feel her climax approaching, and knew by the way the man's muscles tightened beneath her that Kenrick was almost there as well.

Leaning back with one hand holding the sheriff's face against her breasts, Emily reached the other hand back to stroke the side of her hip and flip the skirt away from her thrusting buttocks. Once again, Emily couldn't help but laugh. Her pleasure was growing in intensity, and she bit into her full bottom lip as the first wave of her orgasm swept through her. The lips between her legs clenched around Kenrick's shaft, which seemed to pull a throaty groan from deep within the sheriff.

As he called out, Emily did the same. One of her hands held his neck tightly, while the other went between her legs to rub his pole as it slid inside her. She felt where their two bodies met, and then she reached to the garter strapped to her leg.

With one quick motion, Emily pulled the derringer from its holster, placed it to Kenrick's head, and pulled the trigger, moaning loudly to cover the sharp pop of the gunshot.

Kenrick was still hard when she eased herself back down onto him. The .22-caliber bullet didn't have enough power to go clean through his skull, but it was more than enough to scramble his brains. Emily thought about that as she lowered his head onto the pillows, turning it so that the gaping wound bled straight through to the floor.

While straightening her skirts, Emily slipped the derringer back into its holster. She took another deep breath, noticing how the opium fog was now tainted with the scent of gunpowder. After easing off him, she sat there with Kenrick for another minute or two, pretending to have a conversation and placing the pipe to his cooling lips.

Finally, she got up and fixed her dress. On her way out, she stopped next to one of the Chinese men. "Don't bother the sheriff over there," she said with a wink. "He needs his rest."

THIRTY-NINE

"Well, I'm all for ending this madness," Whiteoak said as they were heading down the boardwalk. "But I'm not sure how good of an idea it is to get everyone together. Near as I can tell, that won't lead to much else besides a bloodbath."

"The blood's already been flowing," Clint pointed out. "And I've already tried taking my time and investigating, only to find out that the blood will keep right on flowing. Now, we've got to get to the source and put a stop to it."

"Then maybe I should sit this one out. . . ."

Clint stopped and grabbed Whiteoak by the shoulder, spinning him around so that he was looking directly into the professor's eyes. "You're the start of this whole damned thing, remember? Now that you've drug me and everyone else into this, you're in it till the end. Besides, there really isn't much else to do."

They'd stopped two doors away from Mil's. The dinner crowd was thinning out, but the smell of roasting meat and baked bread was strong in the air. Clint's stomach had been rumbling for hours, but there simply wasn't enough time to stop and tend to it.

Just as they were about to move on, a thin Chinese man bolted around the corner in a frantic rush. His skin was nearly pale enough to glow in the moonlight, and his breath came in ragged torrents from his lungs. As he sped past the restaurant, the Chinese man felt a strong hand on his shoulder, his momentum nearly taking him off his feet.

"What's going on?" Clint asked after he'd reached out to stop the man.

"The sheriff . . ." he gasped between breaths. "Sheriff dead . . . in my place . . . shot in head . . . he killed!"

"Take me there," Clint ordered.

Glad that someone had taken charge of the situation, the Chinese man turned and led Clint back in the direction he'd come from. It wasn't until they were standing outside the opium den that the panicked man thought to ask who Clint was.

"I'm in town in a matter regarding Sheriff Kenrick," Clint said with an official tone in his voice. "Take me inside and show me where he is."

The slender Chinaman wasn't sure whether he should let Clint inside or run for one of the deputies. Seeing the look of hesitation, Clint began walking inside.

"One of the deputies was also killed tonight," Clint explained as he stepped into the old laundry. "And I'm looking into what happened."

That was enough to rattle the Chinaman so that he put both hands to his head and groaned loudly. "He inside. I show you."

Although Clint was no patron of opium dens, he could certainly recognize one when he stepped into it. Even without the pungent stench of the narcotic smoke hanging in the air, there were plenty of other giveaways such as the piles of pillows on the floor, the chimes and burning incense, and of course the pipes scattered about the room. But except for another older Chinese standing next to the door, the place was completely empty. Then Clint spotted the corpse in the back of the room.

At first, he'd thought the body was just another pile of cushions. In the dim light, it blended in with all the other unmoving objects. Just another shadow with substance. But when he got closer, he could make out Kenrick's face as well as the dark, wet puddle that had soaked all the way down to the floor.

The small hole in Kenrick's head was identical to the one

that he'd seen in the deputy's chest. Also, like the last one, there were powder burns, which told him that the shot had been made at point-blank range. That meant a small gun that had been snuck up close enough to do the job before either man could get to the weapons that were still strapped to their sides.

The first thing that came to mind was a derringer. A woman's favorite kind of gun. Probably favored by strawberry blondes.

Clint walked outside after giving the place a quick once-over. "I've seen enough," he said to Whiteoak, who was waiting for him. "I'm going to pay a visit to someone. I want you to go to the livery. The box is there, buried beneath some hay in the stall next to a big Darley Arabian. Get it and wait for me at the store with the hole in its floor. Be ready for me when I get there, and try to keep your head down. I'm sure there will be plenty of others with their eyes on that place."

Clint watched as Whiteoak took off and headed for a nearby alley. As soon as the professor got near to the alley's entrance, he all but disappeared into the shadows. This was to be the first test of the night, Clint figured. If Whiteoak showed his face again, then maybe Clint had had him figured wrong after all.

Now Clint needed to put the next test into motion.

He went back to Mil's, crossed the street, and went up into the home of Mandy Premont. She wasn't there. Next, he crossed back over to the restaurant and looked around. Again, there was no trace of her. He did, however, find Sam the cook slaving away over a hot stove.

"I need to find Mandy," Clint said through the small rectangular window separating the kitchen from the dining room. "Do you know where she is?"

The Indian didn't even have to think before he answered. "She said she was going to meet someone at the Stone House."

Clint tipped his hat and turned to leave. "Thank you very much." He thought about what Sam had said and how he'd said it. The words had come so quickly from the other man that he must have been ready to say them. So much for that test. Time for test number three.

He remembered passing the Stone House on his way into town. If he hadn't been offered a room with Mandy, he'd been ready to stay at the quaint little hotel. The place looked like it had once been a church, as it was made out of solid gray bricks, complete with the high arched masonry and steeple. The steeple was sealed now, and only one stained-glass window remained.

Clint was admiring that window when the front door opened and Mandy came hurrying outside. "Clint, I'm so glad to see you," she said. When she got to him, she reached up and wrapped her arms around Clint's neck.

"Did you hear about the sheriff?" he asked.

"No . . . what happened?"

"What happened is that he was dealing with the wrong kind of people rather than putting them in jail where they belonged, and he got killed for it. I need you to do me a favor."

"Anything," she said quickly. "If I can do it, I'll gladly try and help you."

"I need you to go home and wait for me. There's something I wanted to see at that abandoned storefront where Owen's body is laying. It should be quiet over there right now, but there may be trouble, and I don't want you to get into any more of it if you can help it."

She pressed herself closer to him and squeezed him as tightly as she could. "What are you going to do?" she asked.

"Since this town doesn't have any law, I'm going to put a stop to all the killing going on here. And I need to start with that tunnel that leads into Mil's."

Mandy pulled herself away and looked up at Clint with a tear in her eye. "Just promise me one thing. Be careful."

Clint leaned down and gave her a gentle, lingering kiss. "Don't worry. I'll see you again." Then he turned and left.

FORTY

Clint circled around town, looking for any traces of the men who seemed to have invaded it for what was beneath it. Sticking to alleys and side streets, he went past the sheriff's office, and spotted two men dressed similarly to the one he'd found inside one of the cells. One carried a Spencer rifle and the other had a pistol.

Moving in a roundabout path, he went past the saloon and opium den. He wasn't really expecting to find much there. It wasn't until he got closer to the spot where Owen Respit's body was that he began to see hints of activity. First, there was the sound of footsteps echoing down the space between the buildings.

It would have been harder to hear them if the rest of the town wasn't doing such a good job of obeying Lee's orders and staying away from that area. Clint crouched down in the shadow of a quiet feed store, and strained his ears for every detail. There were at least three men walking toward the storefront that was also the entrance to the gold-packed cellar.

Clint waited where he was, and watched as Jarrett and Lee came striding down the street, with one of the other black-clad men following behind, then turning and hurrying away.

Suddenly, reflexively, Clint spun around and nearly fired a shot right into Smitty Evanston's chest.

173

Smitty's face was a pale mask of surprise as he held his hands out in front of him palms up. "It's all right, Mr. Adams," he said. "I ain't gonna try nothin'."

Clint kept his hand on his gun and stood up. "Just stay where you are and try to keep your head down."

"But I wanted to see this through to the end. I need to know if I can go back to my normal life and stop hiding."

"Then keep your eyes open," Clint said. "Because the end's on its way."

Clint stepped out of the alley just as Jarrett and Lee had passed it by. When Clint walked into the street, he positioned himself behind Owen's body and squared his shoulders. "Your sheriff's dead," Clint said loud enough to startle both men.

They turned around and started to draw, until they caught sight of who it was that had spoken. The sight of Clint was enough to keep their hands hovering over their pistols, waiting for an opening but not ready to make the first move.

"Yeah," Jarrett said. "We heard about Kenrick. Real shame. Why are you mixed up in this, Adams? You want a piece of the money too?"

"No. I want you to turn yourselves over to me so that I can take you to a real lawman who'll give you what you got coming."

Lee was the first one to laugh. And when Clint heard the click of a hammer being cocked behind him, even Jarrett was forced to smile wickedly. Clint took a step to the side and moved himself around so that he was standing at Owen's feet. From there, he could see Jarrett and Lee out of the corner of one eye, and the strawberry blonde at the other edge of his field of vision. He took a quick glance toward her to check one thing.

"That the same derringer you used to kill Sheriff Kenrick?" Clint asked.

Emily smiled and leveled the weapon at Clint's head. "Drop the gun."

"Looks like we're all here," Clint said as he tossed his pistol to the ground. He then craned his neck to look around at the windows that faced the street. After making a slow, deliberate scan of the area, he raised his voice and said, "All right, Mandy. You can come on out now too."

For a moment, there was silence. Then footsteps came from the storefront that led to the cellar and the door opened upon rusted hinges. Mandy looked scared, and her hands trembled as she kneaded them in front of her body.

"Oh, Clint. I didn't want to leave y—"

"Save it," Clint snapped. "Every damn time I told you where I was going, there was someone waiting there for me with a gun in their hand. It might have been a coincidence if I didn't just happen to run into this little group here at this very moment. Besides, having the tunnel lead up to the restaurant where you work is just a little too much coincidence for me to swallow. Oh, and you might not want to talk so much to strangers if you're going to lie to them next time. Telling me that you were working there just to get out of the house can't be anything but suspicious to someone with their eyes open. That, and the fact that not just you but Mil's cook seems to live better than most people who own places like that restaurant.

"Where is Sam, by the way? Probably keeping a lookout for me to make sure I go where I told you I was going, I'll bet. That's his job, isn't it? To keep an eye on that cellar and anyone looking to get down there. You failed your test, Mandy. Now just shut your mouth before you say something else you'll regret."

As Clint spoke, Mandy dropped the mask she'd put on for his benefit and let the fear melt away from her features. In its place was anger that slowly built into rage. Finally, by the time he was finished, she'd stepped up to him and raised her hand so she could slap him across the face.

Clint's hand was up in a flash, and it caught her wrist with inches to spare. "Why go through all this trouble?" he asked in a low voice. "Why involve others when what you wanted was right beneath your feet?"

Seeing that she wasn't about to talk, Clint moved away from her and looked at the others. Emily was still where he'd left her, holding the derringer pointed at him. Lee and Jarrett had fanned out, spaced equally around Owen's body.

Tension crackled through the air as each person fought with the decision of what they should do next. Clint was

ready to draw the instant he saw someone go for their gun.
At that moment, Clint remembered what Whiteoak had said
about the box of gems and how he'd never told Jarrett about
that particular treasure's existence. That gave him another
idea. "I'll bet you never even told them everything," Clint
said to Mandy.

"What haven't I told them?" she asked sarcastically.

Before Clint could say anything else, another set of footsteps announced the presence of yet another guest around the
body of Owen Respit.

"I think he's talking about this," Whiteoak said as he
tossed the wooden box down at Mandy's feet. Ignoring the
others and paying no mind to Emily's gun, Whiteoak stepped
up to Clint's side.

"What the hell is going on?" Jarrett thundered.

"Tell them," Whiteoak said. "Tell them about what's inside this box that you were going to keep from them." He
then turned to look at Emily. "Or maybe you can."

Emily scowled at Whiteoak. Then she looked at Jarrett. "I
don't know what he's talkin' about, I swear."

But Jarrett's eyes were narrowed suspiciously.

Whiteoak sensed the mistrust, and jumped on it the way
a vulture claimed a piece of dead meat. His hand darted over
to the pocket of Mandy's dress. He then stepped over to
Emily and started circling her. His hand went to her pocket,
snatching something small and shiny. Just as she turned to
point her gun at him, Jarrett's voice rang out.

"Let him be!"

"A wise choice," Whiteoak said. After making his way
back to the box on the ground, he held up his hand and
showed two small keys to the entire gathering. "Now, I'll
give you a look at what you've been missing."

FORTY-ONE

Neither of the women was able to hide the nervousness she felt as Whiteoak got closer to the box holding those keys. When his hand twisted one of them in the lock, the box popped open. He then closed it and did the same with the other key. The second time, however, he held the box open and began to pull back the cover.

Suddenly, the night was alive with voices and movement.

"You'll ruin everything, you son of a bitch!" Emily screamed while taking a shot at Whiteoak.

The professor ducked and dropped down so that he was covering the box with his own body. The bullet from the derringer went wild, and whipped through the air next to Lee's head.

"Holding out on me?" Jarrett screamed as he pulled his gun. "Nobody holds out on me!" Not caring who else was around, Jarrett thumbed back his hammer and aimed at Emily Tate. The pistol barked once and kicked in his hand, but his target had already dropped to the ground with the cool grace of a professional gunfighter.

As the air exploded around her, Mandy started to run back into the store, but was stopped by Clint's hand on her arm. "Let go of me!" she yelled.

"It was easier to let them come in here and take the gold, wasn't it?" Clint said loudly enough to be heard over the gunfire. "Just pretend to help them get their money so they left you with those gems."

Jarrett and the others heard his words, just as they were supposed to. The only one who didn't seem affected was Emily, who was squeezing off another round at Jarrett. A spray of blood erupted from Jarrett's neck.

Grabbing at the wound, Jarrett looked more confused than hurt as his knees began to buckle underneath him. He tried to snarl a few words, but he couldn't gather enough air. So instead, he held his gun up and fired.

Emily's body was spun around in a tight circle, and she went down to land painfully on her side.

Clint still had ahold of Mandy, and wasn't about to let her go. "Is this what you wanted?" he asked. "How much death is worth the price of those stones?"

The look in her eyes, the tensing of her muscles, the way she turned her body, all of it was enough to tell Clint what was coming even before he saw her pull the small blade from beneath the folds of her dress. Clint twisted his body around, trying to keep his eye on where Jarrett and Lee were, as another gunshot exploded from somewhere behind him.

Mandy's head snapped back and her body fell to the floor as though an invisible hand had reached up to pull her down. A fine mist of blood hung in the air, and when Clint turned to look, he saw Whiteoak kneeling over the box with a familiar modified Colt in his hands.

"Here you go, Adams," Whiteoak said while tossing Clint's gun back to him. "You know how to use this better than me."

No sooner did Clint have his gun in hand than he heard Jarrett's voice.

"That money's my future, Adams," Jarrett screamed like a madman.

Clint stood rock solid, waiting for the other man to make his move. He didn't have to wait more than an instant before Jarrett was swinging his gun toward Clint and pulling the trigger. Clint's hand was a blur of motion as he drew and fired, placing a single round cleanly through Jarrett's skull.

The body fell to the ground as Clint was looking around for the other men in black who had come to town with Jarrett. He spotted two of them at the other end of the street. They'd been running toward the gun battle, but when they saw the corpse of their leader hit the dirt, both of them charged forward with guns blazing.

Shots whipped past Clint and Whiteoak, each bullet drawing closer to the mark as the men got nearer. Clint fired once at the man closest to him, and dropped him like a sack of manure. Just as he was about to fire again, he saw the second man already bearing down on him. Suddenly, that man was jerked from his feet as though he'd been tied to a rope that had just run out of slack.

Clint stepped forward, ready for anything. But both men were dead.

"Least I could do for ya," said a voice from the alley across the street. Just then, Smitty Evanston stepped out from the shadows, holding an old pistol in both hands. Smitty turned toward the one man that was left. "I'd rather get shot now than hang for killing Owen."

"You didn't kill Owen," Clint said before any more blood was spilled.

"What?"

"Trust me."

The look on Smitty's face went from desperation to relief. "I didn't kill him?"

Clint shook his head. "No. Somebody else killed Owen."

"I had to," Lee said softly. "He wouldn't give over those deeds. He wouldn't let Jarrett in on the deal. Owen wouldn't do nothin' but keep that money for himself. He was gonna kick me out without a dime to my name."

Smitty stood up straight and spoke with more confidence in his voice than Clint had ever heard before. "Then you're gonna have to answer for what you done. For everything you did to your brothers. I seen what you did to Nickolas."

Without a word, Lee brought his hand up with the speed of a truly desperate man. It wasn't enough to beat Clint, who sent him to hell with one shot.

The street was littered with bodies, old and new. When Clint took a look around, he realized that something was missing. "Where's the blonde?" he asked.

FORTY-TWO

Clint didn't find much of Emily Tate besides a set of tracks
that led to a patch of street that had been walked on so many
times that hers blended in with the tracks of half the town.
Clint figured that Emily would be smart enough to get out
of Chester as soon as possible. There was also one man in
black still unaccounted for. But Clint was too damn tired to
start another hunt.

When he got back, he found Whiteoak with the wooden
box in his hands. Seeing Clint, he pulled his key out of the
lock and stared down like a scolded child.

"Go ahead and open it," Clint said. "You've earned it."

Whiteoak's eyes lit up, and he quickly twisted the key in
the lock. His joyful expression dropped instantly when he
opened the box and got a look at what was inside. His movements slowed by his disbelief, Whiteoak turned the box so
that Clint and Smitty could see the contents.

"Rocks?" Whiteoak said while moving his hand through
the box. Within the felt, there was nothing but rocks that
were just big enough to rattle enough when the container
was shaken. "But . . . what happened to my . . . ?"

Satisfied that Whiteoak had sweated enough, Clint stepped
up and peered into the box. "Oh, didn't I tell you? I didn't
want to take a chance with anyone skipping town on me, so
I hid the gems separately from the box."

Whiteoak's head snapped around. "Where are they, Adams?"

"Relax, Professor," Clint said as he fished something from his shirt pocket. "I believe these belong to you." Clint tossed that something into Whiteoak's hand.

It was another small key, only this one was the one that opened the strongbox in Whiteoak's wagon. As soon as Whiteoak saw it, he clenched it tightly in his fist and let the box fall to the ground.

"Your strongbox is in the stall next to the one where you found that," Clint said. "From everything I've seen, you've got as much right to those gems as anyone else in possession of those deeds. Just take them and try not to get yourself killed."

"Last thing I need," Whiteoak said in an exasperated voice, "is games like this. Jesus, Clint, I nearly felt my heart jump into my throat." He flinched for a second and shook his head. "Sorry. I meant to call you Ad—"

"That's all right, Professor. Clint's just fine."

Watch for

THE SPIRIT BOX

238th novel in the exciting GUNSMITH series
from Jove

Coming in October!

**Explore the exciting Old West with one
of the men who made it wild!**